Chasing Stars

# Chasing Stars

Susanne McCarthy

*And catch a few!*

*Love Susanne*
*xxx*

Chasing Stars

Text Copyright © 2015 Susanne McCarthy

All Rights Reserved

This book is a work of fiction. Names, characters, places and incidents are either the products of the author's imagination or used fictitiously. Any resemblance to actual events, locales or persons, living or dead, is entirely coincidental.

**Cover design by Steve at www.Lazerpics.com**

**ISBN-13: 978-1515172055**

Kat had a very low opinion of billionaire Javier de Almanzor – and that was before he kept her prisoner aboard his fabulous yacht, the Serenity. Javier was the most sinfully handsome man she had ever seen. He was also a low-life scum-bag.

And she was going to prove it.

Javier was intrigued by the beautiful stowaway. Was she a thief? Or just an honest girl trying to get by in the world as best she could. It would probably be safer to return her straight to Antibes.

But who needs safe?

**TABLE OF CONTENTS**

CHAPTER ONE ................................................................. 5
CHAPTER TWO ............................................................... 23
CHAPTER THREE ............................................................ 39
CHAPTER FOUR .............................................................. 53
CHAPTER FIVE ................................................................ 68
CHAPTER SIX .................................................................. 83
CHAPTER SEVEN ............................................................ 98
CHAPTER EIGHT ........................................................... 115
CHAPTER NINE ............................................................. 129
CHAPTER TEN ............................................................... 144
DEAR READER .............................................................. 157

## CHAPTER ONE

"HOI - waitress!" The fat man snapped his fingers. "More champagne over here."

"*Say please*," Kat hissed under her breath, fixing a brittle smile in place as she manoeuvred with her silver tray through the elegant throng.

The champagne was flowing like water, the conversation and laughter growing louder by the minute. The crowded saloon was uncomfortably hot, even though the full-length glass doors at the stern had been folded right back to allow the party to spill out onto the wide aft deck. The golden lights of Antibes sparkled above the marina, rivalling the stars spread across the dark Mediterranean sky.

It was quite a party. If she'd been into celebrity spotting she could have filled a book – seriously A-list movie stars here for the film festival, world-shaking financial moguls, even a smattering of European royalty and a few Arab princes. There were more diamonds than Van Cleef and Arpels, more gold than Fort Knox, and the rock band playing for the dancers on the lower deck had just had their third number one album.

But even more spectacular than the guest list was the yacht itself – the Serenity, one of the largest in the world. One hundred and thirty-five metres of elegant white hull, with a graceful superstructure and six decks, all gleaming pale wood and opulent suede upholstery, bronzed glass and fabulous displays of exotic flowers, and every luxury a billionaire's money could buy.

Ah yes, the billionaire; Javier Francisco Manuel Thiago de Iñiguez y Almanzor. She had done her research thoroughly, poring over the internet for hours. There had been plenty to read – on both the financial pages and the gossip sheets.

His father was a wealthy Spanish landowner, his mother a half-French, half-Lebanese former super-model. He spoke nine languages fluently, including Arabic and Russian. By the age of twenty-two he had exploited that skill to establish himself as a broker in the international oil trade, and now, little more than a decade later, he was reputed to be one of the richest men in the world.

And one of the most eligible. Watching him covertly from across the room, she was forced to admit that he had the looks to go with his playboy reputation.

He really was extraordinarily handsome, with those angled cheekbones and strongly-carved jaw. He was tall – surely several inches above six feet – and the cut of his black dinner-jacket emphasised the powerful width of his shoulders, but he wore it with an air of casual unconcern which underplayed the expensive tailoring.

He held his proud dark head at an imperious angle, like a hawk - an impression heightened by the perceptive glint in those dark eyes. She had caught a close-up glimpse of those eyes as she had passed him at the foot of the steps up from the galley earlier in the evening, and been struck by their colour – the rich, dark brown of espresso coffee, with topaz flecks, and thick black lashes which on a woman she would have been inclined to dismiss as fake.

He was also a sleazy, low-life scum-bag. And she was going to prove it.

It was hot. Javier took a small sip of the mineral water in his glass, listening to several of the conversations going on around him. Were the clocks on strike? The last time he had glanced at his watch – an ostentatious diamond-encrusted monstrosity that he hardly ever wore - must have been at least an hour ago, but the hands had moved barely ten minutes.

A bone-deep ennui seemed to have settled over him as he cast a jaded eye around the crowded saloon. *It's work*, he had to remind himself – not for the first time. If he was doing this for pleasure, he'd probably have thrown himself overboard by now.

In those terms, at least, it had been a resounding success, he acknowledged coolly. No-one turned down an invitation to one of his legendary parties aboard the Serenity.

Like a puppet-master he had gathered many of the richest and most powerful men in the world to drink his champagne and talk business. There were few people who could bring together Baron Leopold Von Henning, the reclusive German industrialist, and Prince Abdul Mansour, in the same room as three top Hollywood film producers.

The luscious blonde at his side was insistently demanding his attention, flashing her doe eyes at him in unmistakable invitation – an invitation he would probably have declined, even if her husband hadn't been somewhere on the boat, probably issuing a similar invitation to some other nubile young beauty.

"If you don't like your hairdresser, why don't you simply go somewhere else?" he enquired dryly – he knew it wasn't the required response, but he was distracted.

Across the room he had spotted the girl again.

He wasn't quite sure what it was about her that intrigued him. He didn't usually pay much attention to the efficient staff who served him – although he hoped he was never rude. Even when they owned a pair of legs that could start a riot - he had caught a thoroughly enjoyable glimpse of them when she had been climbing the aft staircase earlier, precariously balancing a laden tray of champagne glasses.

It was the uniform which jarred; it apparently belonged to someone a little plumper and considerably shorter than her. The top-flight catering agency he always engaged to supplement his own crew for on-board events in Antibes and Cannes usually ensured that their staff were immaculately turned out. And they were usually extremely skilful at manoeuvring through a crowd as if almost invisible.

And they didn't usually pull faces at his guests behind their backs.

He had almost laughed aloud at the searing look she had slanted at that unpleasant sleaze-bag Sir Peter Drummond-Smythe and his equally obnoxious cronies – particularly when one of them had squeezed her neat derriere. He had thought for a moment that she was going to deposit the contents of her tray down the front of his shirt.

But she had returned him a saccharine smile and adroitly moved away – and then poked out the tip of her pretty pink tongue at him when she had thought no-one was looking.

She was quite striking to look at. He had noticed earlier that she was wearing flat shoes – rather worn espadrilles. In an attempt to diminish her height, make herself a little less conspicuous?

It was never going to work. The graceful way she moved would always draw attention, and so would that mop of bright copper curls - she had bunched them into a knot on top of her head, but a few corkscrew fronds were escaping to feather around her face.

Her eyes were the only feature which could be described as conventionally beautiful – a clear grey-green, and fringed with long, dark, silken lashes. In spite of that vivid red hair, her skin was more cream than pale, with just a light sprinkling of freckles over a rather pointed nose. And her mouth was way too wide for her face – though the lips were pink and soft, the colour of wild roses.

But somehow the overall effect was... quirky, and... yes, beautiful.

In sum: as unconvincing a cocktail waitress as he had ever seen. With an almost imperceptible flicker of his eyes he summoned Bob, his head of security, to his side. "The red-head," he murmured, indicating with a brief nod of his head.

Bob picked up on her instantly. "I have her. What's the problem, boss?"

"I'm not sure if there is one. Just a gut feeling. Keep an eye on her - but be discreet. See if she wanders into any part of the boat she shouldn't be in, try to find out if she's working with a partner, even a team."

Bob smiled grimly. "I'm on it."

Javier nodded. If there was anything untoward going on, Bob would discover it. He was ex-SAS, the best in the business – that was why he had hired him, six years ago.

Across the room he watched the girl as she shuffled round a cluster of guests, a small frown of concentration creasing that smooth brow as she precariously balanced her tray of champagne flutes, forgetting to watch out for any guests who wanted to exchange their glasses.

For some reason he found himself hoping that he was wrong – that she was just an innocent, hard-working girl trying to get by in the world as best she could. He didn't want to think she was a thief.

As the full champagne flutes on her tray were replaced by empties, Kat eased her way back to the bar, leaning on it with a sigh of relief. This was hard work – she had a whole new respect for cocktail waitresses.

The bar-steward grinned as he took the tray from her and slid it through the hatch to the wash-up. "Knackered?" he enquired with sympathy.

"Pretty much," she confirmed. "I'm glad I wore flats." She lifted one foot, propping it against her knee as she massaged her aching toes.

"I haven't seen you before," he remarked conversationally. "You're new to the team?"

"Oh… yes. It's just a fill-in really. I've been… hitching along the coast." That much was true – sort of.

"Where are you headed?"

"Oh, wherever.' She shrugged with casual unconcern. "I thought I might go to Italy. Florence, maybe."

He nodded approval. "It's nice there at this time of year. Are you travelling alone, or is there a boyfriend around somewhere?"

She laughed merrily. "No, no boyfriend."

"Ah – that's good."

"It is?"

"Very good," he asserted with a cheeky grin. "If you're not planning to move on right away, maybe we could hook up tomorrow for lunch? I know a great little taverna along the coast that serves fish straight off the quay."

She shook her head in smiling apology. "Sorry, I can't plan that far ahead," she returned lightly, picking up a new tray of champagne flutes and plunging back into the throng.

As she moved discreetly around the room, she was careful to avoid Javier de Almanzor's eye-line – the last thing she wanted was to attract any attention to herself.

It wasn't difficult – he was surrounded by a clutch of admiring women, fluttering their fake eyelashes at him, hanging on his every word. All designer dresses and designer tans, Kat designated them with a touch of asperity. Didn't he ever get bored with all that adulation?

Apparently not, to judge from the endless paparazzi shots of him she had found on-line - arriving at a premier or leaving a nightclub with a succession of jet-set beauties on his arm, the daughters of rock stars and half the aristocratic houses of Europe, it seemed, as well as the usual contingent of actresses and models.

Not that the images she had viewed on the small screen of her cell-phone had really done him done him justice, she acknowledged reluctantly. He was simply the most sinfully handsome man she had ever seen.

And nothing could have prepared her for the sheer impact of his charisma. It went way beyond mere good looks – it seemed to charge the space around him like some kind of magnetic force-field, drawing all attention to him without him making any apparent effort.

Ah, the power of money, she mused dismissively. Truth be told, he'd probably had plastic surgery to clean up that jaw-line, and Botox injections to keep the crows' feet at bay. And she'd just bet he had a personal trainer to chivvy him along in the gym.

But she could understand why her young step-sister had succumbed to that practiced charm. Amy was just nineteen years old, and had always been carefully protected by her doting father – Kat's step-father.

She had met Javier de Almanzor on the ski-slopes in February, and by Easter she was pregnant – and her gallant lover had promptly disappeared. And with him her cell-phone, with all the photographs of them together and all the text-messages they had exchanged – all the evidence of their relationship.

A heartbroken Amy had tried to contact him many times, but all she could get on his cell-phone was voice mail, and all her emails had gone unanswered. It was quite obvious that he intended to deny ever having had anything to do with her.

But he had reckoned without Amy's step-sister, Kat vowed fiercely. Amy's father had been a better father to her than her own had ever been. She had been heartbroken when he had died two years ago, but she had promised herself then that she would do her best to repay his kindness by taking care of Amy.

She was going to get that cell-phone back. And then she was going to force Javier de Almanzor to accept his responsibilities...

"Phew, don't these people ever go to bed?"

Kat started back guiltily – she had been hovering at the top of the stairs which led down to the lower deck where the staterooms were situated, waiting for an opportunity to slip down unnoticed.

"All I want to do is get my feet into a nice bowl of hot water," the other waitress sighed. "These new shoes are giving me blisters."

"Mmmm," Kat murmured uneasily – she didn't want to risk getting into conversation with any of the other agency staff if she could help it.

"You're new?" the other girl enquired.

Kat nodded.

"You're supposed to wear your name badge," the girl reminded her, tapping her own – Kat could see that she was called Juana, and she was a supervisor. Dammit!

"Oh... I... don't have one yet," Kat temporised quickly. "I only signed up with the agency this morning."

"And they've put you on a job already? Without any checks?"

"My cousin works for them, so they said it would be OK." A couple of days ago she would never have believed she could become such a fluent liar, Kat reflected wryly. "And they were short for tonight."

"Tell me about it!" Juana conceded, rolling her eyes. "Ah well, make sure they get you a badge for your next job. And a better-fitting uniform, too," she added, glancing down at Kat's skirt, which was far too short, even though it was settled on her hips instead of her waist – she was all too aware that it was revealing a considerable length of her slim legs.

Kat hoped her smile didn't look too false. She hadn't signed up with the agency at all – in fact, until this afternoon she'd never even heard of them.

She had been loitering discreetly on the quayside at Port Vaubun, watching the comings and goings on the decks of Javier de Almanzor's spectacular yacht and wondering how on earth she was going to get aboard unseen by the burly security guards on duty, when a minibus and a big black truck bearing the logo of a high-end catering agency had turned in through the gates and drawn up right next to her target.

As she had watched, a huge hatch had been lifted at the stern of the yacht, giving access to a well-lit hangar-like space on the lower deck, and the uniformed catering team had piled out of the minibus and began to unload dozens of boxes and several large stainless steel catering trolleys from the back of the truck, and convey them onto the yacht.

It was too good a chance to miss. Strolling casually past the minibus, she had spotted a pile of spare uniforms on the back seat. Without giving herself time for second thoughts she had slipped inside and picked one that more-or-less fitted, ducking below the windows as she had wriggled into it and stuffing her own clothes beneath the seat.

And then she had simply tagged onto the back of one of the big trolleys, pretending to help trundle it across the gangplank and through the service hatch to the lower deck level of the yacht.

Her heart had been in her mouth the whole time – she was gambling on the hope that the catering crew weren't a regular team who all knew each other. But after all, what was the worst that could happen? She might be thrown off the yacht, maybe even get arrested, but she wasn't actually committing a crime – well, maybe trespass, but that was a civil matter.

But it seemed that the uniform had rendered her virtually invisible. No-one in the catering crew, nor any of the security guards, had given her a second glance. After that, she had simply joined in quietly with whatever the catering crew were doing, and no-one had questioned her presence.

Juana sighed, and glanced at the colourful plastic watch on her wrist. "Well, I suppose we'd better start getting some of these glasses collected up," she remarked, moving away.

"Yes. I'll… just check around downstairs then, shall I?" Kat suggested brightly. It would be the perfect excuse! "People have been up and down all evening."

The other girl murmured some vague acknowledgment, too busy with her own task to even notice what Kat had said, and Kat snatched at the opportunity to dart down the wide curving staircase to the lower deck.

Javier's cell-phone purred discreetly. He drew it out of his pocket and glanced at the screen. "Bob?"

"She's headed downstairs," came the security chief's gruff voice.

"OK – keep watching," Javier responded quietly. "If she's just collecting glasses, that's fine. But if she tries to get into my suite... activate the security over-ride."

There was a second's hesitation on the other end of the call. "You sure boss?" Bob queried.

"Yes. But once she's inside, make sure she doesn't come out."

A soft chuckle, and the line went dead.

It was much quieter down here, but every bit as fabulous as the upper decks – all light wood and cream carpets, and discreetly recessed lighting. There were paintings on the walls – brightly-coloured abstracts that looked like originals - and a lingering scent of beeswax beneath the aroma of cigar smoke and stale alcohol that permeated the air.

There were five doors on each side of the corridor, and several stood open to display opulent staterooms. People were still milling around, collecting mink wraps and Prada bags, and laughing tipsily as they sought their way back to the upper decks. Kat wouldn't mind betting that there were a few thousand dollars' worth of white powder still dusting the glossy tiles in some of the luxurious en-suite bathrooms.

But fortunately there were also a few empty glasses to justify her presence. She moved around silently, avoiding eye-contact, her head dipped slightly – apparently the discreet servant, but in reality so that there was less chance of anyone seeing her face and being able to describe her later.

She had a rough idea of the layout of the decks – she had looked it up on the internet, and although she had only been able to find a few external shots of the Serenity she had found a similar one built by the same yard, and had studied it with care. So far it had panned out.

This whole deck was given over to sleeping quarters, with the ten guest suites, just as she had expected. And at the far end, beneath where the for'ard stairs divided to climb grandly to the deck above, there was a pair of double doors, which stood closed. The master stateroom.

Pausing at the last of the empty guest suites she left the glasses she had collected on a small table just inside the door, and peered cautiously out into the corridor. A couple, somewhat the worse for wear, were weaving their way unsteadily towards the aft stairs, but they had their backs to her, and anyway they were probably in no fit state to notice anything.

Moving silently, she slipped across to the double doors. Of course they would probably be locked... With a last swift glance back over her shoulder she put her hand on the polished brass handle, and turned it cautiously.

Miracle - it wasn't locked!

Very carefully, she eased the door open.

Within half a second she was inside, the door closed behind her, her heart pounding so loudly that she was sure they would be able to hear it on the upper deck, even over all the noise of laughter and conversation and music. But there was no alarm, and slowly she began to breathe again.

The room was just stunning. It filled the full width of the boat, and the long windows on three sides let in a surprising amount of light reflected up from the shimmering water – enough to get a general impression of her surroundings, anyway.

To one side of the room was a lounging area, with comfortable suede-upholstered sofas around a long onyx slab of coffee table, and a large plasma television screen fixed to the wall. Wide glass doors led out onto a private fore-deck – if the Serenity was indeed identical to the yacht she had seen on the internet, that deck would be accessible only from this room, and would have its own Jacuzzi.

Two low steps curved across the room, elevating an area which was partially screened off by a bronzed glass partition patterned with a gold Mondrian-style design. Beyond, on a raised dais was a huge circular bed, covered in a satin quilt of a rich teal blue which matched the curtains and the cushions, a strong accent to the acres of ivory carpet and glossy ivory ceiling.

For a moment she paused, just gazing around. This was Javier de Almanzor's lair – a faint hint of something spicy and very masculine lingered in the air, conjuring the vivid image of the man himself. And suddenly her heartbeat was fluttering, her head felt light, her body warm - almost as if he was there beside her, that charismatic presence overwhelming.

It was crazy – she had never even spoken to him, and yet she could feel the lure of those strong arms, those dark, mesmerising eyes. The man ought to carry a government health warning – a naïve young thing like Amy would have been a lamb to the slaughter.

Which brought her attention sharply back to her task.

Of course there was no guarantee that he had kept Amy's cell-phone, but she had to look for it. The second possibility was the distinctive purple ski-suit he had been wearing in the blurry selfies Amy had sent her from the ski-slopes – if she could find that, and photograph it here on the yacht, that would prove a link.

So... where to begin?

There was a low table on each side of the bed – it was worth trying those first, Kat decided swiftly. She had kept her own cell-phone in her pocket, and using its LED light as a torch she searched both the tops of the tables and the narrow drawers beneath. But there was nothing useful – a Kindle, a half-eaten tube of mints, a couple of motoring magazines...

With a sigh of exasperation she glanced around the room again. The other yacht had had a spacious en-suite bathroom and dressing room – this one was bound to have the same. But where...? Ah, of course – the door was discreetly concealed within the gleaming beechwood panelling that lined the wall behind the bed.

A sound outside the door made her catch her breath in panic – but it was only someone using a vacuum cleaner. They were unlikely to come in here, but still...

The light from her phone gave little help to find the door handle, but skimming her fingertips down the wall revealed a discreet brass plate embedded into the wood panelling, and as she pressed it there was a soft click and the door swung silently open.

She stepped inside and closed the door quietly behind her. At least if the cleaner did come in she should be safe in here. A fragrant hint of... cedarwood? teased her nostrils. It was pitch dark, but she wouldn't risk turning the light on – the light from her cell-phone would have to do.

The dressing room was spacious. Each side was lined with full-length louvered cupboards, and beyond was an opulent bathroom lined in glossy black marble, with gold taps, a shower that could comfortably hold four people, and a bath the size of an Olympic swimming pool – well, nearly.

Heavens, you could hold an orgy in here...

But she wasn't going to find anything useful in the bathroom, she reminded herself firmly. Quickly turning back to the dressing room, she opened the first door. Inside was a stack of neat shelves of cashmere sweaters, and in spite of her hurry she couldn't resist running her hand over them – so soft, so warm...

Unexpectedly an image flashed behind her eyes, of Javier de Almanzor wearing one of these sweaters, its softness a beguiling contrast with the hard-muscled body beneath as he casually tugged it off over his head to reveal a lean, sun-bronzed torso...

Javier's cell-phone purred again; Bob. "She's in the master suite."

So – she was a thief, after all. A common thief. He felt little satisfaction in being proved right. But that was the only reason she would have gone in there. If she had been a commercial spy – the other possibility which had occurred to him – she would have tried for his office, up on the bridge deck.

"OK. Where are you?"

"In the corridor outside - with the vacuum on. She won't risk coming out while she knows she'll be seen."

"Excellent. Stay where you are. I'll be down shortly."

At long last his guests were drifting away, staggering their way along the quayside, where a string of fancy cars were waiting to bear them away. In a couple of hours it would be dawn.

The staff from the catering agency were moving around with their usual quiet efficiency, tidying up. He had used them for a number of years, and usually they were completely reliable. But something had gone wrong tonight – and he was about to find out what.

Moving across the saloon, adroitly disentangling himself from all the people who wanted to thank him rather tipsily for 'a simply *wonderful* party, dahling – yours are always the very *best* parties of the season' he made his way to the for'ard stairs down to the lower deck.

All was quiet down here, except for the quiet hum of the vacuum cleaner – a neat trick, that, keeping her effectively trapped without her even knowing they were onto her. Bob grinned, and signalled a thumbs-up. Javier returned him a grim smile, and with a deliberate rattle of the handle pushed open the door of his suite.

Kat stiffened. Someone was coming into the stateroom! Quick as a flash she slipped into one of the cupboards and pulled the door shut behind her, easing herself silently to the floor and pulling the row of shirts across in front of her, hardly daring to breath.

The lights came on in the main room. She could hear whoever it was moving about, whistling softly to himself. She hardly dared to breathe. And then the footsteps came closer, the dressing-room door swished open, and through the slits in the louvered door she could see a pair of very expensive handmade leather shoes, and the lower part of a pair of elegantly-tailored trousers.

Javier.

He paused very close to her hiding place, and as she watched he eased off the shoes, opening a cupboard next to hers and stashing them on a shelf. Then the trousers appeared, as he stepped out of them and neatly put them away too. Oh no – the shirt! But as she peered out from her hidey-hole, she saw the shirt and the socks bundled up and tossed carelessly into another cupboard – there must be a laundry basket in there.

And then as she watched, a pair of navy-blue silk jersey boxer shorts followed them. Kat felt her mouth grow suddenly dry. He was standing there stark naked, just inches from her face. And she was trapped. How on earth was she going to get away now? All she could do was wait and hope that he would soon go to bed, and that he was a heavy sleeper.

Her search for evidence was over.

The disappointment knotted inside her – she had been so close! But worse was the fear of discovery. She was beginning to get cramped in the awkward space – all that was needed now was that she would need to sneeze... No, don't even think about that!

Cautiously she eased her left leg into a slightly more comfortable position – Javier had disappeared into the bathroom, and the next moment she heard the sound of the shower running. Could she risk trying to slip out while he was in there? Biting her lip hard between her teeth, she slid a finger into one of the louvers of the door, and opened it barely half-an inch.

Oh my gosh! He was in the shower, barely six feet away from her. His back was turned towards her, and he was completely naked, the water splashing down over his smooth golden-bronze skin. Hard muscles rippled across his wide shoulders and in ridges down his back as he vigorously scrubbed his body with a large sponge - down over tight, firm buttocks, and long, strong thighs.

She couldn't stop herself staring – he was magnificent.

And then he began to turn, and she pulled the cupboard swiftly shut, closing her eyes. There were some things that it just wasn't wise to see – she'd never get a good night's sleep again! She heard him whistling softly, heard the shower stop, and a few moments later his bare feet padded past her hiding place. Oh please, let him be going to bed.

But it seemed he had other plans. The next thing she heard was a woman's voice, speaking French. He had a visitor...? No – it was the television. Surely he wasn't going to sit there watching it for long? It must be four o/clock in the morning, at least!

He seemed to be flicking through the news channels – she heard a cultured English accent, then American, then one she didn't understand but guessed from the background music that it was probably Arabic.

At least she could let herself breathe, though she was getting more and more uncomfortable, her knees bent almost up to her chin. And she was tired – she had been travelling all day, and then had been working for hours serving champagne to his obnoxious, pampered friends. All she wanted to do was sleep...

The thought brought an inevitable yawn, almost dislocating her jaw. Just sleep...

Her mind drifted, half in dreams. Snatches of images – the spectacularly beautiful harbour, with it shoals of luxury yachts moored at the quayside... trundling a catering truck along a brightly-lit passageway on the lower deck of the Serenity... peeping out from her hiding place as she watched Javier in the shower...

Dammit, she didn't want to think about that. The last thing she needed was to let herself be sidetracked from her objective by Javier de Almanzor's undeniable physical magnetism.

Poor Amy may have fallen for it, but she was seven years older, and knew a little more about men. She had even been engaged once... Well, almost. But nevertheless she wasn't nearly as naïve as her young step-sister.

How easily Amy been fooled. Javier had even been subtle enough to realise that such a young, innocent girl might have been intimidated by the full-on power of a billionaire playboy in his thirties. He had come on to Amy as if he was much closer to her in age and experience, and wealth, pretending that they had so much in common.

Lies, lies, lies.

Maybe if she had been at home while all this was going on, she would have been able to intervene before disaster struck. But she had been in New Zealand, escorting parties of adventure tourists on white water rafting expeditions on Rangitikei River. She had been following the budding romance through Amy's regular texts – right up until that last despairing message that Javier had vanished.

She had fixed up with a local tour guide to cover for her, and had been on the next flight home.

After doing her best to put Amy back together, and taking a few hours to do a bit of research, she had been on her way again. Her first attempts had met with little success. She couldn't even get past security at his apartment in the swankiest part of Barcelona, and the prestigious office-block which housed the offices of the *Sociedad Limitada de Almanzor* had been even tougher.

But a trip to the family chateau in the foothills of the Pyrenees had yielded a useful snippet of information, courtesy of one of the gardeners who had been impressed by her knowledge of the varieties of New Zealand flax.

She had found out that Javier tended to spend most of his time on his yacht, using it as a base for his high-octane brand of business networking. And that the yacht was currently moored in Antibes, where Javier would be throwing one of his spectacular parties.

It had taken her a whole day to hitch-hike along the coast. The friendly lorry driver who had brought her from Marseilles had shown her a nice little pension, cheap but clean, where she had booked a room and left her back-pack, and then she had gone down to the marina to reconnoitre.

And there her luck had finally changed – or at least she had thought so at the time…

A merry jingle in her pocket jerked her back from her reverie. Frantically she snatched up her cell-phone and jabbed at it to silence it. He had the TV on – maybe he wouldn't hear it…

No chance. The door of the dressing room opened, the light came on, and the sound of a soft, husky laugh set the hairs on the back of her neck on end.

"So, would you like to come out now, or are you planning to stay in there all night?"

## CHAPTER TWO

KAT JERKED in shock at the sound of that sardonic voice, jolting her elbow against the cupboard door, knocking it open. Losing her balance she tumbled out, sprawling in an undignified heap on the floor, her cell-phone skittering away to come to a stop against Javier de Almanzor's foot.

He stood in the doorway of the dressing room, laughing in lazy mockery. Fortunately he had a towel wrapped around his waist – not that that was much help, she reflected, struggling to catch her breath. That wide, tanned chest, scattered with a few rough, dark, curling male hairs over the ridges of hard muscle, could do very odd things to a girl's sanity.

Those dark eyes, as rich and brown as expresso coffee, were regarding her with a glint of amusement, and she realised that her skirt – already far too short – had ridden up further to reveal a good deal too much of her slender thighs. Grasping the hem, she tried in vain to tug it down a little. A slow smile of appreciation curved that hard mouth.

"Welcome aboard the Serenity, Miss...?"

She felt a thud of panic. She couldn't risk telling him her real name – she wasn't sure if Amy would have spoken about her in so much detail, but if he recognised the name it would definitely mean the game was up. "Smith," she responded, her throat tight. "Miss Smith." Dammit, was that the best she could come up with?

"Miss Smith." The way he arched one dark eyebrow eloquently conveyed that he had no trouble at all in guessing that she was lying. "Don't you think that's a little formal, under the circumstances?"

"I don't believe we need to be on first name terms," she retorted crisply, struggling for some semblance of dignity – not easy, when she was sitting on the floor at his feet. "I won't be staying."

"Oh – what a pity." He held out his hand to help her up. "I hoped we might have a chance to get to know each other."

"I don't think so, thank you." She ignored his hand, scrambling somewhat inelegantly to her feet.

Those expresso-brown eyes slid over her in mocking appraisal. "Well, Miss... ah... Smith, perhaps you'd like to explain what you were doing in my dressing room?"

Kat was struggling to steady the racing beat of her heart. It wasn't because of *him* – of course it wasn't. Even though he was drop-dead gorgeous...

It was simply the shock of being discovered, anxiety about what he might do. Would he hand her over to the police? If he did, there would be little chance of her ever again getting close enough to him to get the evidence to prove that he was the father of Amy's baby.

Those beguiling dark eyes were watching her, waiting for an answer to his question; she was pretty sure that he wasn't the sort of man who would tolerate being kept waiting long. "I was... hiding," she blurted out a little desperately.

"Oh? Pardon me, but that seems to be quite obvious," he pointed out, infuriatingly sardonic. "The interesting aspect would be from whom, and why?"

Kat tilted up her chin, attempting to regain some semblance of dignity. "If you must know, I was hiding from one of your sleaze-bag guests," she retorted, calling upon that hitherto unsuspected capacity for lying through her teeth. "He kept trying to paw me, so I came in here to get away from him. When I heard someone at the door... Well, I thought it was him, so I... hid."

Oh dear – that had sounded almost plausible, until the last bit. But it was the best she could come up with on the spur of the moment – she was just going to have to brazen it out.

Javier regarded his uninvited guest with interest. It was almost a convincing excuse – he might even have swallowed it, if he hadn't already suspected that the sweet innocence in those wide grey-green eyes was utterly deceptive. But he wasn't going to let her know how much he already doubted her – not yet.

"And which of my guests was it who was causing you such distress?" he enquired in a sweetly solicitous tone.

Her eyes flickered briefly to the right and back again – she might be a prolific liar, but she wasn't a particularly convincing one. "I... don't know," she claimed, tilting up that pretty chin. "I didn't stop to ask his name."

"Describe him," he persisted – watching her embroider her story was proving unexpectedly amusing.

"Fat guy." She had clearly become aware of his appreciative appraisal of those spectacular legs, and tried to shimmy her ill-fitting skirt a little lower – did she realise just how provocative that movement was? "Bald. Wearing a dinner jacket."

Javier smiled dryly. "Hmmm – that could describe several dozen of the gentlemen here tonight. But no matter. Why did you not make your presence known when you realised I was not he?"

"I didn't know who it was," she insisted. "I couldn't see you – I could only hear someone moving about."

"You didn't hear the shower?"

"Ye-es..." she conceded carefully.

"So you must have known it was me. Who else would be taking a shower in the owner's suite?"

"How was I supposed to know who owned the boat? I was just here to serve the drinks." She shrugged her slim shoulders, a movement which drew his attention to the round perfection of her small breasts beneath that ill-fitting uniform. "For all I knew it could have been the fat guy. Anyway, now that I know you're not him, I can get back to work."

As she moved to step past him, he blocked her escape with his arm. "So eager to get away?" he taunted softly.

He had mentally acknowledged that there was a third possible explanation for her presence. It had happened before

– a rather crass attempt to get into his bed, with an eye to a lucrative kiss'n'tell story in the down-market press.

Unfortunately for the young women who tried it, he wasn't inclined to fall for it – and even if he had, there was little money to be made: he wasn't married, he wasn't a politician, he wasn't even much of a celebrity. As one editor of his acquaintance had cynically remarked, *'Rich Playboy Sleeps With Attractive Girl'* - where was the story in that?

Besides, she didn't seem the type.

For a start, she didn't seem to be wearing more than the very minimum of make-up – the kiss'n'tell brigade were usually covered in inches of slap, under the mistaken impression that it made them more alluring. And they were usually pretty brazen in their approach – they wouldn't stand there looking like a startled faun at the sight of him wearing only a towel around his waist.

Of course, there was one sure way to find out. Offer her an open opportunity, and see if she took him up on it.

He smiled slowly, and put up his hand to coil one finger into a long copper curl that had fallen from the loose knot on the top of her head. "Don't rush off," he coaxed, infusing his voice with a smoky note of seduction. "We've barely got to know each other."

Her reaction wasn't quite what he had expected. Her hand rested briefly on his wrist, almost a caress… And then abruptly her grip tightened, and with a swift movement she shifted her balance - and he found himself lying flat on his back as she fled through the door.

Kat raced up the stairs to the main saloon. She had been afraid that someone would try to stop her, but there was no-one around. No-one…? But she didn't have time to consider the significance of that minor detail as she fled across the empty saloon and out onto the aft deck…

And crashed into the rail.

Aghast, she stood staring out at the easily-recognisable flood-lit façade of Fort Carré and the lights of Antibes, receding into the distance, already more than a mile away across the smooth, dark expanse of the Mediterranean.

Javier de Almanzor's sardonic voice came from behind her. "I really don't think things are so bad that you need to throw yourself overboard," he taunted.

She turned sharply. Javier was leaning casually against the door of the saloon. Fortunately he had thrown on a navy-blue silk dressing gown, knotted loosely around his waist, but he was smiling with a lazy mockery that made her itch to slap his smug face.

"Take me back," she demanded furiously.

He shook his head. "I'm afraid that would be... inconvenient."

"Inconvenient?" she repeated, her eyes flashing fire. "Why? It would only take a few minutes to turn back."

"We would miss the tide."

"Oh, don't be ridiculous," she snapped. "A boat this size wouldn't have to be bothered about the tide along this coast."

He acknowledged her point with a sardonic nod. "Very well. I don't see why I should put myself to any inconvenience for a stowaway."

"I'm not a stowaway," she protested hotly. "I told you, I was hiding from one of your guests."

"Oh yes." His voice had hardened, and she felt a small frisson of fear shiver down her spine. "A guest whom you are unable to describe with any degree of accuracy."

"I wasn't paying him much attention," she countered, clenching and unclenching one hand in agitation – as she realised what she was doing, she quickly hid it behind her back. "I just wanted to get away from him."

"Of course," he conceded, his voice clearly conveying the message that he didn't believe a word of it. "Well, whoever he was he's gone now, so you're quite safe. Perhaps you would care for a drink?" The look she returned him made him laugh, and he held up his hands in a gesture of innocence. "Oh, don't worry – I've learned my lesson. You'll be quite safe with me too."

"I don't want a drink." She was glaring at him in angry defiance, those fine blue-grey eyes flashing fire at him. "I want to go back to Antibes."

"And so you shall." Javier was unable to keep the note of mocking amusement out of his voice. "On my return."

That stopped her in her tracks. "Your return from where?" she queried edgily.

He waved his hand in an airy gesture – really, who could blame him for winding her up? "Wherever I decide to go. The Greek islands, perhaps, or the Black Sea – it's very nice there at this time of year."

She stared at him in blank shock. "But… how long is that going to take?"

He shrugged in a gesture of lazy unconcern. "Oh, a month – maybe six weeks."

He heard her sharp intake of breath. "You think I'm going to stay on this boat all that time?" she demanded heatedly. "Put me off at the next port you call at."

"Do you have your passport on you?" he enquired with a bland smile.

"N… No," she conceded reluctantly.

"I didn't think you did. I can hardly land you in some random country, with no passport and no money, now can I?"

That stumped her, but only for a moment. "I can go to the British Embassy," she tossed back at him in triumph.

He shook his head decisively. "Questions would be asked. That may cause me some delay."

"Oh, heavens," she drawled, her hands on her hips, her voice rich with sarcasm. "Far be it from me to cause you any delay."

"Quite." He was enjoying this. Not just the attractive flush in her cheeks, the ragged breathing that was making those nice little breasts flutter beneath that oversized shirt, but the sheer entertainment of having her stand up to him, argue with him – that was a real novelty. "So, you may as well come and have a drink, while we talk."

He stood aside from the doorway into the saloon, gesturing politely for her to precede him. She hesitated, her white teeth biting into the softness of her lower lip – he would like to try that, just to see if those lips tasted as sweet as they looked.

But she knew she had no cards to play, and he watched with grim satisfaction the moment she conceded defeat.

The elegant saloon was in darkness, and looking rather the worse for wear, still littered with the debris of the party – a few half-deflated balloons drifting forlornly into corners, trails of curling streamers in untidy piles under chairs, overflowing ashtrays and plates of half-eaten canapés, and glasses still stained with the dregs of the champagne left forgotten in odd corners when the guests had wandered off to dance or mingle.

Kat hesitated in the middle of the room as Javier passed behind her and walked over to the bar, flicking on the lights to create a pool of intimacy that seemed to cut them off from the rest of the world.

Outside was nothing but inky night, the lights of the coast now a distant glow on the horizon. There was no sound from the engines, and the movement of the boat was virtually undetectable – no wonder she hadn't known that they had left harbour when she had been hiding downstairs in that cupboard.

"So what can I offer you to drink?" Javier enquired. "Champagne?" He hiked an unopened bottle out of a bucket of melting ice.

She wrinkled her nose in distaste. "Ugh. I've smelled enough of that tonight to last me till next Christmas. I'll just have a glass of water."

"Sparkling or still?"

"Oh... er, still, please."

"Ice and lemon?"

She eyed him warily as she settled herself stiffly on one of the upholstered bar stools. "Yes please."

Her mind was racing. How was she going to get out of this one? Stuck here on this yacht, maybe for weeks? Amy would be going frantic! But she couldn't let this man know what was going on in her mind – at all costs she must keep up a cool façade, keep her secrets hidden.

"You've missed your vocation," she remarked as he tonged several ice-cubes into a tumbler and deftly cut a wafer thin slice of lemon, then poured a bottle of mineral-water over the top. "You'd be a natural behind a cocktail bar."

That temptingly firm mouth curved into a smile of sardonic amusement as he slid the tumbler across the bar to her. "Thank you," he responded dryly, taking a brandy snifter from a high shelf and lifting it to the row of optics on the back wall. "I'll remember your careers advice if I should ever be so unfortunate as to need it."

Kat could feel that odd fluttering beat of her heart again, a kind of excitement – similar to the feeling she got when she was launching a raft at the top of a white-water run, or preparing to leap off a bridge a dizzying height above a raging torrent with only a length of bungee rope around her ankles to break her fall. A kind of fear mixed with anticipation.

Which was ridiculous, she scolded herself firmly. She had no reason to be afraid of Javier de Almanzor – she had already proved that she could handle him perfectly well if the need arose.

And she certainly had nothing to anticipate. Just because he was drop-dead gorgeous. And simmeringly sexy...

Well, yes, OK – he was. Of course he was. She could acknowledge that as a fact without it necessarily having anything to do with her. What he had done to poor Amy was quite enough to inoculate her from falling under his spell.

She could regard him with the kind of dispassionate fascination she might feel for a beautiful but deadly yellow-belly – she had seen one of those in an aquarium in Brisbane, but she had no desire whatsoever to encounter one up-close and personal.

He had had his hair trimmed since Amy had taken those selfies, and the designer stubble was gone. On the whole, she maybe preferred this look – those sculpted cheekbones and hard jaw could have been carved by Michaelangelo.

Taking a sip of her iced water, she settled herself a little more comfortably on her bar-stool and forced herself to meet his eyes. "So, what was it you wanted to talk about?" she enquired, politely distant.

"You."

"Me?" She shrugged her slender shoulders in a gesture of unconcern. "There's really nothing to talk about."

"We could start with your name," he suggested.

"I told you my name."

"Ah yes. Miss Smith. No first name."

"Miss Smith is good enough," she retaliated defensively.

"Very well, Miss Smith," he conceded, a hard note creeping into his voice. "Let's go over this again. What were you doing in my suite?"

She tilted up her chin – if she was absolutely honest, she *was* a little afraid of him, but she wasn't going to let him think he could intimidate her. "I told you – I was hiding from your sleazy friend," she insisted.

"Really?" He arched one dark eyebrow in cynical enquiry. "And yet you appear quite capable of looking after yourself - as I found to my cost." He rubbed his left shoulder with a slightly rueful grin.

"Are you saying you would have wanted me to deposit one of your fine guests on his lardy backside?" she challenged defiantly.

He laughed at that – a rich, dark, velvet sound like the low notes of a cello. "Perhaps not," he conceded. "But you can see why I may find your story somewhat… dubious."

"Not at all." It was just hunger that was making her feel light-headed, she assured herself firmly. And lack of sleep, after a long day hitch-hiking from Barcelona, then serving drinks to his fancy friends. "But if you choose to see it that way, that's up to you."

"So tell me," he continued smoothly, "where do you come from?"

"England."

Those dark eyes flickered with something dangerous. "The last I heard," he responded, his voice warning her that his patience was wearing thin, "England has an area of over fifty thousand square miles, with several dozen large cities and thousands of towns. Where exactly, in all of that extensive geography, are you from?"

"Why do you want to know?" she challenged uneasily.

"Why don't you want to tell me, if your presence on my boat is as innocent as you claim?"

Dammit - cornered. "I come from London," she conceded, recognising when it was wise to retreat from an untenable position. "Peckham." She didn't choose to mention that for the past fifteen years home had been her step-father's pleasant country mansion in Surrey.

"And what sort of work do you do?" he continued. "If you have a job?"

"Oh, this and that," she dismissed airily. "A bit of office work, sometimes." Well, the front desk in the offices of the adventure holiday agency she had set up with a couple of friends.

"Current employer?"

She arched one finely-drawn eye-brow, taking a sip of her mineral-water to give herself time to think. "I wasn't expecting the Spanish Inquisition," she responded lightly.

"No-one ever does."

So, he had a sense of humour, at least, with that subtle take on the hackneyed Python quote. *Stoppit* she warned herself sharply – *don't start looking for good points. Remember who he is, what he did. And for goodness' sake try to remember what lies you're telling, so you can keep your story straight.*

Her attempt at diverting him from his interrogation hadn't worked – he was still waiting for a reply, that dark, level gaze far too perceptive for comfort. "I was temping mostly." She smiled with what she hoped was an air of casual dismissal. "Lots of places – I couldn't possibly remember them all."

"Surely you remember the name of the agency you worked for?"

"A… Agency?"

"Yes. Usually temps are recruited through an agency. Which one did you work for?"

*Oh heavens – think of something, quick…* "It was just a small one. Near London Bridge. You wouldn't have heard of it."

"There's no need for me to have heard of it - I can have my people check out that you are who you say you are. Though I admit that an enquiry regarding a 'Miss Smith of Peckham' is unlikely to yield very helpful results," he added on a note of dry humour.

Kat couldn't find it amusing. *'His people.'* Of course, he would have a whole squadron of 'people' at his beck-and-call. At some point maybe she should have considered just what a formidable opponent Javier de Almanzor could turn out to be, if she hadn't let herself be so swept along by her determination to sort everything out for Amy.

Maybe at the point when she had realised that she wasn't dealing with a scapegrace twenty-something trust-fund baby, but a powerful and ruthless thirty-something billionaire commodities broker.

But it was a bit late now for second thoughts, she acknowledged wryly. She had made her bed… No, that wasn't the analogy she wanted lingering in her mind right now…

"On the other hand," Javier continued, faintly menacing, "I could check with the catering agency."

"I… wasn't actually working for them." Her mind raced, swiftly spinning a new story that might sound at least remotely plausible. "Not officially. My friend… wanted to see her boyfriend – he's going back to America tomorrow, and they wanted one last night together before he left. But she didn't want to risk losing her job by not turning up, so… I stood in for her."

"And her name…?"

She shook her head, her jaw set. "I don't want to get her into trouble."

That sardonically raised eyebrow mocked her for wasting her breath – he knew that she had been lying with virtually every word she had uttered.

"So, you're Miss Smith. You weren't working for the catering agency, and you don't feel inclined to tell me who you do work for, or indeed where you live. Given all that, and the fact that you were stowing away on my boat…" He raised an elegant hand to cut off her argument. "Please, spare me that silly story – I didn't believe it the first couple of times I heard it, and I'm even less inclined to believe it now. Given all of that, I really think I would be quite within my rights to have you confined to the brig."

Kat stared at him in shock. "You don't have a brig on a yacht," she protested, her voice unsteady.

"I can assure you that we most certainly do," he responded, the hard note in his voice a subtle threat. "It's generally used as a storage room, I believe, but we occasionally need to press it into service if a member of the crew gets a little too drunk, or we happen to pick up some pirates."

She laughed in frank disbelief. "Pirates? Now you *are* having me on."

"Not at all," he responded with a cool smile. "We captured a pirate boat three years ago, off the coast of Somalia. I think they got a bit of a shock when they tried to attack us. They weren't expecting us to be so heavily armed."

"Armed?"

"Of course. We sail in international waters. You can't just ring the police and get a nice swift squad car to turn up if you get into trouble."

Kat rolled her eyes - she would hardly be surprised if he told her he had a nuclear warhead ready to rise up from some concealed compartment beneath the swimming pool!

"I must admit, however," he went on, his voice like silk wrapped around ice, "it's probably not very pleasant down in the brig. I'm told it can get rather hot, and tends to smell of carbolic soap."

"Oh, wonderful!"

"There may be an alternative," he offered, those dark eyes glinting with enigmatic amusement. "You could work your passage."

She slanted him a suspicious glare from beneath her lashes. "As what?" she demanded with little regard for grammar.

"I'm sure we could always use an extra hand on the domestic side."

"Cleaning your toilets, you mean?"

"Heads."

"I beg your pardon?"

"On a yacht they're called heads," he explained smoothly. "But I imagine it would be preferable to the brig."

"And those are my only two options...?"

He smiled slowly, one dark eyebrow raised in mocking question as he allowed his appreciative gaze to slide down over her, lingering on every inch...

"OK," she conceded, almost choking for breath. "I'll crew for you."

The sardonic glint in his eyes left her wondering what he would have done if she had hinted that she might have been willing to accept that unspoken third option. Oddly, she wasn't one hundred per cent certain that he would have taken her up on it.

And even more oddly, that thought left her feeling as deflated as one of the left-over balloons drifting silently across the floor of the saloon.

"Excellent." He smiled like a snake. "You can sleep in one of the guest-cabins for now, and in the morning I'll arrange for the Chief Stew to allocate you a crew-cabin."

Javier stood on the private foredeck outside his stateroom, watching the first grey streaks of dawn creep above the eastern horizon, turning the sea to mother-of-pearl. It had been a most successful evening, in financial terms — introductions made, deals proposed which would be of mutual benefit.

And each of the parties would want him to conduct the negotiations, trusting his reputation for absolute honesty.

Which would make him… a great deal of money.

A wry smile curved his firm mouth. He'd probably ring his mother later — he usually spoke to her every few days — and he could almost hear her reaction to the news. *'So, you've made a few more millions. But are you happy?'*

Bless her, she was always worrying about him, her wayward younger son. When he was growing up, she had always been the one to come between him and his father in their many spats. They were too much alike, she had always told them.

Was that true? He swirled the brandy in his glass, watching as the long, low rays of the rising sun touched it with a luminous gold. He had always thought of his father as arrogant, obstinate, so fiercely proud of his family heritage.

Well yes, he acknowledged with a touch of self-deprecating amusement: arrogant and obstinate - guilty as charged. But that noble family heritage had most often been the main bone of contention between them. Don Francisco de Almanzor had demanded that his sons carry on the family traditions, slaves to the family estates and vineyards.

Javier had always argued that he could safely leave that privilege to his older brother Edgardo – dutiful Edgardo, as proud of the family wine label as their father. Already he had produced the required heir, and some to spare, fathering two lively sons and two pretty daughters with his beautiful, eminently suitable wife.

But fond as he was of his little nieces and nephews, Javier had never had the least desire to emulate his brother - he really couldn't see himself settling down to a life of cosy domesticity. Even just a few days spent at home in the vast, gloomy halls of the Casa del Almanzor was enough to have him longing for freedom.

Besides, with whom? Into his mind drifted the mental image of a long line of all the women he had dated over the years; his mouth quirked into a crooked smile as he acknowledged that it was a very long line.

Maybe there was something wrong with him, he mused, taking a sip of the brandy and enjoying its velvet caress as it slipped over his tongue, leaving a lingering hint of spicy oak. Each and every one of those women had been undeniably beautiful, intelligent, and well-bred - and yet after no more than a few weeks he had found himself growing restless, frustrated... bored.

Bored with laughter that was too eager to treat his mildest touches of humour as the wit of the century. Bored with talk of diets and shopping and the latest facials and Botox treatments. Bored with the parties and premières with all the same faces, the same petty gossip and fixed smiles.

Oh, the relationships had mostly ended amicably enough – he was still friends with most of his ex-s. And it wasn't that he didn't believe that marital bliss was achievable – his parents were an excellent example of that, and so was his brother.

It just seemed that it wasn't for him.

Suddenly he burst out laughing. "Dammit, what are you doing feeling sorry for yourself?" he demanded aloud. "It's a beautiful dawn on the open sea, you own the most beautiful yacht in the world, you can afford to buy any damned thing you want. Get a grip, *imbécil*."

Downing the last of the brandy he strolled back into the master stateroom, shaking his head as he shrugged off his silk robe. The movement caused a slight twinge in his shoulder where he had fallen hard on the floor when his beautiful stowaway had thrown him so neatly across her hip.

Now that was one woman who might prove interesting to get to know, he reflected as he tossed back the covers and climbed into bed. He couldn't imagine her earnestly agreeing with every word he uttered, even when he contradicted himself, or changing her plans at the last minute to fall in with whatever he wanted to do.

Unfortunately getting involved with her was probably not a good idea, he reminded himself firmly - at least not until he found out a little more about who she was and what she was doing stowing away on his boat. Starting an affair with her could lead to all sorts of unwelcome complications.

## CHAPTER THREE

KAT woke with a start at the sound of a knock on the door, and had called, "Come in," before she was fully awake. Slightly dazed as she gazed around her, she realised that she was in a wide, comfortable bed in a luxurious room. It was unfamiliar, but there was something more than that which struck her as odd about it – one of the walls seemed to be slightly curved...

The door opened, and a tall woman with neat blonde hair, wearing a crisp white shirt and well-tailored olive-green culottes, stepped into the room. "Good morning," she greeted her briskly, crossing the room and throwing back the curtains to reveal a brilliant blue sky beyond the row of large windows along the curved wall. "I'm Maggie – the Chief Stewardess."

Memory returned rapidly – smuggling herself onto the yacht, hiding in the dressing room... Javier de Almanzor... in the shower...

"Señor de Almanzor said to let you sleep in for the morning, but if you want some lunch now you'd better get dressed and come down to the crew mess," Maggie went on, dropping a pile of clothing on the end of the bed. "Here's your number two uniform. It should fit OK – I'll sort out your number ones later. If there's anything else you need, you can get it from the stores – we can deduct it from your wages."

"Uh... Thank you," Kat managed to respond. She'd be getting wages? Blinking against the brightness of the sunlight streaming in through the windows, she sat up in the bed and hugged her arms around her knees. "What time is it?"

"Almost noon," came the brisk response. "I'll send one of the girls up to fetch you in half-an-hour to show you the way."

Kat could tell by the level look she slanted at her that the Chief Stewardess was burning with curiosity about the mysterious appearance of a young woman whom she had been instructed to add to the crew roster, but she was far too professional to ask questions.

She was gone as briskly as she had arrived, leaving Kat to try to get her head on straight.

She looked around, taking stock of her surroundings. She was in one of the smaller guest cabins, on the same deck as the main guest suites but further towards the stern.

Not that it could be called cramped, she reflected dryly – as well as the large bed there was plenty of room for a dressing table and writing desk unit built into one corner, and a cream-coloured leather sofa built into the other, scattered with satin cushions of a soft minty green that matched the curtains and the bed cover.

No luxury was spared for all of Javier de Almanzor's guests, apparently – though she would imagine the crew cabins were unlikely to be as well-favoured.

Javier had brought her down here after their discussion in the saloon. She had been a little nervous as she had preceded him down the stairs, wondering whether she had called it wrong. She had thought he wasn't interested in trying to get her into bed, but what if…?

After all, even if she didn't know what a notorious playboy he was, what had happened to Amy would be warning enough. And there had been no sign of anyone else on the boat – though it was the middle of the night, there must be crew somewhere, but she had no idea where. To all intents and purposes, they were alone.

But he had been the perfect gentleman - close enough for her to feel a tingling electric charge between them as he had opened the door of this guest room for her, but never actually touching her.

And the mocking glint in those dark eyes had told her that he was well aware of the confused jumble of fears and emotions running through her mind. He was a man who knew women well, and knew well the effect he had on them.

*Stop thinking about him.*

At least as one of the crew she was unlikely to have much to do with him, she assured herself. With luck, she would simply fade into the background, as unnoticed as one of the pot plants. Well, she'd try, anyway.

So – time to get up and get moving, find out what her new 'job' was going to entail. And face her new colleagues, who were going to be as curious as the Chief Stewardess about what she was doing here. Drawing in a long, deep breath, she rolled out of bed.

The view from the window was amazing. There was nothing to see but the sea - blue sea, a vivid sapphire blue, beneath a cloudless sky of the same pure shade, and so dazzling that it hurt her eyes to look at it. Sunglasses were clearly going to be essential – maybe she could get a pair from the 'stores' and add it to the bill to be deducted from her wages.

The en-suite bathroom, though rather less opulent than the one in Javier's suite, was luxurious enough, all marble tiles and gold-coloured taps, with a roomy shower and a well-lit mirror above the double-sink vanity unit. The familiar reflection staring back at her, wearing the underwear she had slept in, was standing hands on hips, a slightly crooked smile curving her wide mouth.

"Well, here's another fine mess you've gotten yourself into," she remarked, Oliver Hardy style. She was stuck here on this boat, for heaven only knew how long. She had lost her cell-phone - left behind in Javier's dressing room - so she had no way of getting a message to Amy or her mother.

Oh, they probably wouldn't worry too much – often when she was on her travels she was out of contact for weeks at a time, in places where there was no internet, no cell-phone signal. Though Amy might feel a little hurt that she had apparently disappeared, abandoning her when she was in such a mess – she hadn't told her what she was planning, in case she didn't succeed.

Which was probably just as well, she reflected wryly - it didn't look like she was going to succeed now. Javier was suspicious of her, she would be watched – she wasn't going to get the chance to search for Amy's stolen cell-phone or the purple ski-suit, or anything else.

No, dammit – she wasn't going to give up that easily. She had been a fighter her whole life. Bullied at school before it was discovered that she was dyslexic, not stupid, she had fought back with fists and feet and fingernails, been excluded from three different schools and on several occasions brought the police to her mother's front door.

It was her step-father who had sorted everything out, soon after he had married her mother, sending her to a small, quiet private school where her reading problems had been solved with a few simple techniques, and encouraging her learn martial arts to channel her aggression.

That was why she had promised that she would always look after Amy. So somehow she would find a way to get the evidence that would force Javier de Almanzor to at least acknowledge his child. After all, she had managed to get herself onto his boat, and though she was pretty sure that she would be watched, she couldn't be watched *all* the time.

All she had to do was wait – an opportunity would be bound to turn up sooner or later.

Stripping off her bra and pants, she stepped into the shower. It was well supplied with bottles of shampoo and conditioner, and shower-gel – all top brand names. Well, she might as well enjoy the luxury while she could, she reflected, sniffing the exotic scent of jojoba and African cacao extract before pouring a generous dollop into her hand and rubbing it into her hair.

It was the bane of her life, her hair. No matter what she tried to do with it, it remained a mass of wild ginger curls. Usually she tried to keep it under control by fixing it into a knot on the crown of her head, but there were always a few strands that got away.

Along with her dyslexia, it had been a source of more bullying at school. She'd been called everything from Beaker to Ronald McDonald, told her hair looked like a rusty brillo pad, and even been asked leerily if the carpets matched the curtains – she'd been innocently confused by that one when she was twelve years old, which had caused even greater hilarity among the older boys who loved to bait her until she lived up to the stereotype of the fiery-tempered red-head.

But in the present circumstances it could be a distinct advantage, she mused, rinsing out the shampoo and rubbing in the silky smooth conditioner. She wasn't Javier de Almanzor's type at all.

If the images of him she had tracked down on the internet were a fair indication - not to mention all those diamond-bedecked princesses clustered around him last night - he went for sleek, sophisticated creatures, groomed to perfection, every artfully-tumbled curl carefully placed, every inch of skin buffed and tanned.

And then there was Amy, who couldn't be described as sophisticated at all. But she was so pretty that any man would be attracted to her, whether she was his 'type' or not. Unfortunately that lack of sophistication had apparently encouraged a predator like Javier de Almanzor to take advantage of her. But clearly he had only ever been looking for a diversion – he would never have been serious about her.

And now he was looking for a diversion again, pretending to flirt with Kat herself, letting that arrogant gaze linger for rather too long on her legs, as if she was supposed to be flattered by that. But if he thought he could fool her as easily as he had fooled Amy – and heaven only knew how many other young women – he would soon find out his mistake.

Besides, he wasn't her type. A filthy rich playboy, swanning around on his fancy yacht, throwing wild parties… He might be as handsome as sin, but that didn't impress her. She was more interested in what went on between a man's ears than whether he had a pretty face.

Not that you could call Javier de Almanzor *pretty,* she acknowledged judiciously – his features were finely sculpted, but strong and uncompromisingly male. And his body…

But she didn't need to be thinking about that right now, she scolded herself resolutely. She had to think of a way of getting into Javier's state-room again to find the evidence she needed – without arousing any more suspicion.

"Do you have any information about her yet?" Javier leaned back in his black leather office chair and swung his feet up easily onto the corner of his desk.

His head of security shook his head grimly. "Not yet. The catering agency couldn't shed any light."

"I'm not surprised at that," Javier mused. "She's already admitted that she didn't work for them."

"No-one there is admitting to even knowing her. But they found some clothing in one of their mini-buses. It seems likely she slipped onto the bus when it was parked on the quayside and stole one of their uniforms, then mingled with the catering team to get on board the yacht."

"And no-one spotted her?"

"The catering team are mostly casuals – they don't necessarily know each other. Once she was in their uniform they would just have assumed she was one of the team. Same goes for our own crew, unfortunately. I'm sorry, Javier – they slipped up badly there. It was a mistake that shouldn't have been allowed to happen - there's going to have to be some tightening up."

Javier shrugged those wide shoulders in a gesture of casual dismissal. "These things happen," he remarked. "There's no need for heads to roll."

Bob accepted the comment with a grateful smile. "I've put the word in with the *Gendarmerie* at Antibes," he went on. "They'll let me know if anyone answering her description is reported missing. But I suspect she's a bit of a drifter – maybe even sleeping rough. The best hope is that someone will find any baggage she's stashed somewhere, maybe even her passport, and hand it in, but I'm not optimistic."

"Well, I'll leave that to you."

"Are you sure it's a good idea to keep her here on board?" Bob queried anxiously. "It might be safer to turn her in to the police right away."

"Safer, perhaps," Javier acknowledged with a wicked grin. "But far less entertaining."

Bob frowned. "You just be careful," he exhorted with concern.

"You think she may be dangerous?" Javier enquired lightly.

"One way or another."

Javier laughed. "Don't worry – I'll be keeping a close eye on her. A very close eye," he added with a contemplative smile.

"What a mess! These rich nobs certainly know how to party."

Kat gazed wryly around the vast saloon. In the bright sunlight of a Mediterranean afternoon it looked even worse than last night, with food crumbs on the floor and sticky rings on the marble tables. A few drifting strands of blonde hair-extensions, a couple of odd shoes, a discarded silk pashmina...

"Ah well, the sooner we get started the sooner we get finished," her companion added cheerfully. "We'll sweep the floor first, and clear off the tables as we go. You do that side and I'll do this."

"OK."

Kat took the big broom that Gill was holding out to her. Already, after the luxury of the guest stateroom, she had come right down in the world when Gill had shown her the crew cabin they would be sharing, with its bunk beds and low ceiling, its tiny porthole and its narrow en-suite bathroom.

Now she was kitted out in her 'number two' uniform - an olive green tee-shirt with the name of the yacht, '*Serenity,*' embroidered in gold thread above her left breast, and loose cotton shorts in the same colour. Downstairs in the crew cabin were her 'number ones' – smart olive green culottes and a crisp white shirt with short sleeves, and an olive green silk floppy bow-tie – to be worn when there were guests aboard.

Seen in daylight, without the crowd of guests, Kat was able to get a much better impression of the yacht. At this level, part of the deck above was cut away in a long oval, accessed by the wide sweeping curve of an open-tread staircase. With full-length windows on both deck levels, it created a bright, airy space, enhanced by the pale wooden floors and ivory hide upholstery.

From where she was standing, in the middle of the vast main saloon, she could see the whole length of the boat, from the sharp white bow cleaving through the sunny blue waters of the Mediterranean, to the pale wooden aft-deck and the curved stern rail above the long white trail of wake churning up behind them.

"Gosh, it's beautiful," she breathed, gazing around.

"It is, isn't it?" Gill agreed as proudly as if she owned the boat herself. "And it'll be even better when we've finished clearing up. Come on, all these tables have to be polished."

Javier leaned back in his chair with a weary sigh, running his hand back through his crisp dark hair. He had rarely read a more boring financial report. The bright sunshine and the deep blue sea beckoned - what was he doing, wasting his time stuck in his office trying to make sense of endless columns of figures, on such a beautiful afternoon?

He rose to his feet and strolled across the room, and out onto the deck aft of his office. Down on the lower decks the crew were busy restoring the yacht to its usual pristine condition. He leaned his hands on the rail, and drew in a deep breath of salty sea air to clear his head.

He loved the sea in all its moods. Today it was as smooth as silk beneath a hot blue sky, but he loved it equally when it was storm-dark and roiling with white-caps, or a windswept grey-green – the colour of...

Unbidden the memory of a pair of wide grey-green eyes, fringed with long silky lashes, rose in his mind.

That girl again. She was quite a distraction. If he was honest, she was the reason he hadn't been able to give his usual concentration to that damned report. He kept thinking about the way those bright copper curls feathered around the vulnerable nape of her neck... about those long, long legs in that short, short skirt...

And as if the thought had conjured her, there she was – leaning over the rail, shaking out a couple of dusting cloths. As she disappeared back inside the saloon, he found himself walking down the steps and following her.

The domestic staff had been busy in here, he noted as he paused on the threshold. Two large black plastic sacks in the middle of the floor stood up by themselves, bulging with collected rubbish. All the plates and glasses that had been abandoned last night had been whisked away, all the smears and ring-marks had vanished from the tables.

She was there, on her hands and knees, polishing the brass trim at the base of the for'ard guest lift. Her crew uniform fitted her rather better than that catering team outfit, he mused, studying with the appreciation of a connoisseur the way the green cotton shorts moulded over her neat derriere. It was tipped pertly in the air as she bent to her task, rocking backwards and forwards in way that kicked him sharply in the solar plexus.

He strolled slowly across the room, continuing to blatantly admire the view – no red-blooded man could resist it. She heard his footsteps, and twisted her head to look up at him.

"Good morning," he greeted her, indulging himself with a smile of mocking amusement. "You seem to make a habit of being on your knees at my feet."

Her response was barely audible, but it didn't sound very polite.

"Are you enjoying the voyage?" he persisted, deliberately goading her – he so much enjoyed crossing swords with her when she was angry.

"You can't imagine how much satisfaction I get from polishing brass," she bit back acidly.

"I'm pleased to hear it."

"I was lying."

He laughed. "That seems to come very easily to you."

She sat back on heels, shrugging her slim shoulders. Yes, that uniform fitted her very nicely indeed – he already knew that she had a great pair of legs, now he could better appreciate the firm ripe swell of her small breasts beneath the soft cotton jersey of her T-shirt.

"Lying, or polishing brass?" she retorted, slanting him a sardonic glance.

"You have very sharp tongue," he accorded, untroubled by her barbs. "That could be unwise, given the position you're in."

"You mean kneeling at your feet?"

"That too," he conceded. "But don't forget, I could still hand you over to the police as a stowaway."

Those fine grey-green eyes flashed like cold steel. "I might have guessed you'd be the type of man who would break your word if I failed to be sufficiently grateful for the opportunity to clean up after your delightful guests," she rapped scornfully. "Did you know that one of them threw up in the Chinese Fan Palm?"

He frowned sharply at that. "No, I didn't," he conceded. "You had to clean that up?"

"Well, I didn't think there was much point in leaving it for you to do it," she returned dryly. "Besides, it made it stink in here." That neat little nose wrinkled in distaste. "We had to get rid of it before we could do anything else."

Now she had succeeded in making him feel guilty – how had she done that? "My apologies on behalf of my guest," he said, turning on his most charming smile.

"Apology accepted," she returned tersely. "Now if you don't mind, I have work to do."

"I thought you might like to have coffee with me," he suggested. "To make amends?"

"Amends for what? Kidnapping me? Calling me a liar? Or just the vomit?"

"All three?"

She sat back on her heels, regarding him with cool disdain – quite an achievement, from that position. "Do you usually invite your junior crew to have coffee with you?"

"Er... Not usually, no," he conceded.

"Ever?"

"Alright, no - not ever." Had there ever been a more impossible woman? "But you're not exactly the usual kind of crew."

"That's exactly what I am," she insisted decisively. "At least until you see fit to return me to Cannes. And as such, I'm afraid I must politely decline your invitation. As I said, I have work to do."

And with that she turned her back on him and resumed her polishing, making it abundantly clear that the conversation was at an end.

"My gosh, what on earth were you talking to Javier about?" Gill's friendly face was alight with curiosity.

"The disgusting behaviour of some his guests," Kat responded lightly.

Gill giggled. "No really," she protested. "I heard him invite you to have coffee with him."

"Well... yes," Kat conceded.

Gill sighed. "I wish it had been me. Well, no I don't really," she corrected herself wryly. "Jean-Pierre probably wouldn't like it. And I think you were right to say no." Her grey eyes were earnest. "I've known crew girls who've got themselves involved with boat owners – it's never a good idea. They just want some entertainment – at the end of the voyage they can't dump you fast enough."

"Don't worry," Kat assured her with a grim smile. "I've no intention of getting involved with him. Not after…"

"After what?" Gill queried, curious.

"Oh, nothing." She shook her head. "I just know his type." She stretched to ease her aching shoulders, and glanced around. "What else is there to do in here?"

"We've pretty much finished," Gill concluded. "We just need to bring the rugs and cushions back up, and the plants. They're down in the main store. I'll show you the leisure deck on the way – we're allowed to use it, so long as Javier or any of his guests aren't in there."

The leisure deck was aft of the accommodation deck, as Kat had learned to call the deck where the guest suites were situated.

"This is the cinema," Gill announced, opening the door to show her a room with several banked rows of comfortable armchairs, facing an enormous cinema screen. "There's stacks of DVDs, whatever you fancy. This is the hair salon and massage room. Hi Cathy," she added to the young woman inside who was folding a large pile of towels. "Just showing Kat around."

"Hi." Kat offered her usual friendly smile, but the lukewarm response warned her that she was held in suspicion by most of the crew.

"Don't mind Cathy," Gill murmured as she closed the door. "This is the gym."

She opened a door on the other side of the passage. It was one of the most well-equipped gyms Kat had ever seen – runners, rowers, bicycles and weight machines, a squash court and a Jaccuzzi. Most five-star hotels would envy such extensive facilities.

"And we've got a swimming pool," Gill announced with pride, indicating the glass doors at the end of the room. "It's empty at the moment, of course – while we're underway. But when we drop anchor it can be filled in less than half an hour."

"Wow!" The pool on the aft deck beyond the doors was large, lined with tiles as blue as the Mediterranean which sparkled in the sunlight streaming in through the retractable glass roof. At one side there was a swim-up bar, with three stools.

"This is the best yacht I've ever worked on," Gill enthused. "Loads of people want to sign on as crew." She slid a sideways glance towards Kat. "A lot of people would be dead jealous if they knew you'd jumped the queue."

"It... wasn't quite like that," Kat protested weakly.

Gill smiled. "OK, I promised I wasn't going to ask questions," she conceded. "Anyway, come on – let's get finished up with these cushions, then we can take a break."

The helicopter swooped in to land on the upper deck, and Bob jumped out, ducking low to avoid the still-spinning rotors, then reached back into the cabin and pulled out a pink canvas back-pack. A moment later he strode into Javier's office and dumped the back-pack on the floor.

Javier swung his chair around from his desk. "Well done," he accorded genially. "What did you find out?"

Bob put his hand into the back-pack's side pocket, and drew out a passport. "Her name's Kirsty-Ann Tennison. British - and pretty widely travelled."

Javier took the passport and leafed through the pages, studying the numerous visa stamps on the pages. "She certainly gets about," he conceded dryly, turning to the photograph and studying it with interest.

The date of issue of the passport indicated that it had been taken three years ago. She had worn her hair loose, and it curled around her head and tumbled over her shoulders like a halo of bright copper. Considering the matter carefully, he really wasn't sure if he preferred it like that, or scooped up in that nonsensical top-knot she wore it in now.

Maybe the top-knot – that would give him the pleasure of taking it down…

"Twenty-six years old," he calculated, glancing at her date of birth. "Anything else?"

Bob shrugged his beefy shoulders. "The catering agency definitely knew nothing about her. They found these in their mini-bus, stuffed under the seat." He produced a pair of skimpy denim shorts and a pink T-shirt. "She was reported missing by a small *pension* – cheap place, popular with backpackers. She only checked in there two days ago, said she'd be back for supper – but she didn't show up. When she still hadn't appeared by this morning, they phoned it in."

"They were quick," Javier remarked, taking the discarded clothes from Bob and examining them. Those denim shorts… he'd certainly like to see her in those…

"They've had some concerns about some dodgy-looking characters hanging around, bothering the female guests."

Javier laughed dryly. "If any dodgy-looking character tried bothering her, I wouldn't give much for his chances," he remarked.

Bob slanted him a questioning look.

"She had me flat on my back within the first five minutes," Javier confessed. "I never even saw it coming."

Bob frowned. "Are you sure it's safe to keep her on board?" he queried anxiously.

Javier laughed again. "Safe? Maybe not," he conceded. "But who wants safe?"

## CHAPTER FOUR

IT WAS hot in the galley - the pot-wash didn't even have a porthole. As the newest member of the crew, Kat acknowledged that it was probably only fair that she had drawn the short straw on the day's duty roster.

But there was something deeply satisfying about scrubbing the pans. With each one, she was visualising Javier's face in the grease, and scouring it vigorously with wire wool.

Gill had told her that the crew mess was one of the best of any boat she'd worked on. Spacious and airy, it had a large-screen television and a pool table, as well as its own gleaming galley and a long dining-table where they had all sat for dinner last night.

The crew seemed like a nice bunch – mostly young, and from half-a-dozen different countries. There had been lots of laughing and joking during the meal, and they had made her feel welcome. She had been a bit concerned that there might be awkward questions, but though she had sensed their curiosity, no-one had said a word about her unusual arrival on board.

She had kept her ears pricked for any snippets of information about Javier which might be useful, but he hadn't been mentioned.

At last the final pot was clean and put away. Kat wiped down the draining board, and hung up the cloth where she had been shown. With a wide yawn, she stretched her back, easing the muscles in her shoulders.

She had never minded hard work, but she hadn't had much sleep in the past couple of days, and she had always hated been cooped up in small spaces like the galley. But she had a couple of hours off now – it would be a relief to snatch the chance to go up on deck.

The sky and sea were still that glittering turquoise blue, with not a cloud in sight – the only mark on the sea was their own white wake churning in a long streak of foam behind the stern. The huge yacht felt like a tiny speck, as if they were caught in the centre of a vast blue diamond.

Kat breathed deeply, grasping the rail and leaning back to let the cool salt-tanged air fill her lungs.

Suddenly something caught her eye – a long narrow shadow across the wooden deck from something on one of upper decks. She tracked it upwards; it was the blade of a helicopter.

Edging along the deck, she was able to see more of the machine. It was painted in a gleaming dark green livery, the same colour as the crew's uniforms, with a swirl of gold writing; *Almanzor SL*.

Not just a casual visitor then.

Anger surged inside her, and prompted by the impulse of the moment she raced up the steps to Javier's office on the bridge deck. She swung the door open without even bothering to knock.

Three men were inside; one of them in a white shirt with pilot's epaulettes on the shoulder, the second she recalled seeing hanging around at the party.

And Javier. He was leaning back in a big leather executive chair, his feet resting casually on the desk. The other two glanced round at her precipitous entrance, startled, but Javier was as cool as ever.

"Ah, Miss… Smith. What can I do for you?" he enquired, impeccably polite.

"You have a helicopter."

He glanced out of the window to where it sat on the aft deck, feigning surprise. "Good gracious, yes - so I do."

She was not amused. "It could take me back to Cannes."

"Why would I allow that?" he enquired. With a slight inclination of his head, he indicated to the other two men to leave them alone, which they did, closing the door behind them. "Would you care to sit down?" he invited cordially. "Or do you prefer to quarrel standing up?"

"You acknowledge that I have grounds for a quarrel, then?" she demanded.

"No - merely that it's fairly obvious you're intending to have one."

"I certainly am," she blasted at him. "Why are you keeping me here?"

"I want to know what you were doing hiding in my dressing room," he responded, as cool as she was heated.

"I... told you." Her voice wavered slightly – it wasn't easy to lie smoothly when those compelling dark eyes were locked on hers.

He shook his head chidingly. "Maybe you could try telling me the truth. Your name isn't Smith, for a start." He opened a drawer and produced her passport, arching one dark eyebrow in sardonic enquiry.

"Where did you get that?" she demanded, holding her hand out for it.

He laughed, twitching it out of her reach. "There was something of an upset when you failed to return to the hostel. Bob – my head of security – has certain... useful contacts in the local *gendarmerie.* They gave him the tip-off, he paid your bill at the *pension* and collected your belongings."

"Oh..." She drew in a long breath. "So – you know my name." But apparently he hadn't made the connection with Amy - at least that was a bit of luck.

"I know your name. What I'd like to know is why it was necessary for you to use a false one. I warn you," he added on a note of deliberate menace, "I can find out everything about you, from where you went to school to your bra size."

"Then go ahead," she retorted, her eyes flashing fury. "I have a pile of greasy baking trays to wash." And with that she slammed out of the office as noisily as she had entered it.

The only time Kat saw Javier over the next few days was from a distance. They were moored in a sweeping bay a little way south of Rome, with tall cliffs to one side and a pretty fishing village nestled against the shore.

The helicopter came and went a few times - sometimes Javier was in it, sometimes he wasn't. Sometimes there would be various people in expensive business suits, clutching briefcases, who would vanish into his office up on the bridge deck, where the helicopter landed.

Sometimes lunch would be served there, sometimes they would come down to the magnificent dining room, which had been restored to its glossy perfection since the party. With its long windows on three sides, looking out over the long curved bow of the boat, the views were stunning.

With just a few visitors, and none staying on board overnight, the work of keeping the boat up to the pristine standards insisted on by Maggie, the Chief Stew, only took a couple of hours each day.

The deckhands were taking the opportunity to sand and varnish the main deck, but for a good part of the time the multi-national crew could sunbathe, play deck-games, or dive off the swim-platform at the stern of the yacht and splash around in the warm Mediterranean Sea.

But Kat found sunbathing boring – she preferred to make use of the state-of-the art gym. An hour on the exercise bike or rower could burn off a good deal of the excess energy and frustration caused by her lack of progress towards finding the evidence to help Amy.

She was enjoying a comfortable five kilometer run on the treadmill when the door opened and Javier walked in. Her heart, which was already beating fast from her workout, thumped and began to race, and she missed her footing on the treadmill belt and almost fell off the back of the machine.

She managed to catch herself without looking too much of a klutz. Forcing herself to breathe steadily, she switched the machine off, picked up her water bottle and swung her towel onto her shoulder.

"Don't let me interrupt your workout," Javier drawled, barely concealing his amusement.

"I've finished."

"Or scared?" he taunted.

She glanced back at him, ultra-cool. "Why should I be scared?"

"Why indeed? Perhaps because you have something to hide?"

She shrugged her slim shoulders in a gesture of casual dismissal. But she didn't want to give him grounds to accuse her of running away, so she flicked the switch on the treadmill and stepped smoothly onto the belt.

This time she set it a little faster than before, in the hope that the vigorous exertion would distract her from his presence. But as he settled down on the rower next to her she realised that there was little hope of that.

He was wearing a sleeveless yellow T-shirt that seemed to be moulded to his sculpted torso, and loose dark blue cotton shorts. Hard muscles moved beneath sun-bronzed skin as he propped his feet into the rests and grasped the handles.

Kat watched, almost mesmerised as he drew in a deep breath, filling his lungs, and hauled back on the handles.

It was a struggle to keep her attention on her running. The pace usually wouldn't present her with any difficulty, but she was finding it really hard to focus.

She tried turning her head to look out through the porthole beside her to the wide blue horizon stretched out beneath the clear blue sky, but she was far too conscious of the man to her right, of the sheer power in that hard body as he bent his back into the rower.

Images shimmered in her head, of him standing naked in the shower. Those images had taunted her far too often these past few days.

What was going on with her? She knew what he was – but even armed with that warning, somehow she still couldn't deny the wicked temptation to let herself imagine what it would be like… What it would be like to feel those strong arms around her, to surrender herself to his kisses, to tangle with him skin to skin on that big bed in his stateroom…

No – dammit, this had to stop. She had got herself onto this boat with a purpose, and that purpose wasn't to end up as another one of Javier de Almanzor's many conquests. Surely she could exercise a little self-control?

It wasn't as if she was completely naïve when it came to men. Well, OK, maybe she couldn't quite claim to be a woman of the world, but she'd had her share of boyfriends – some of them even quite serious.

But sex, lust… whatever, had never been a high priority for her. And now was not a good time for that to change.

Javier was enjoying the physical challenge of trying to beat his own best time on the rower – the small screen in front of him showed his pre-programmed target performance as a moving red icon, while his current performance was represented by green. Already he was feeling the warm vibration in his muscles, the sweat beginning to break out down his spine.

But if he had hoped it would take his mind off the presence of the gazelle-like creature running beside him, he was soon proved wrong.

She had been a distraction since he'd first spotted her, the night of the party, half-way up the steps from the tank deck - though he really was at a loss to figure out why. Sure, she had a fabulous pair of legs, and the rest of her was put together pretty nicely, too.

But feisty red-heads with impressive martial arts skills were not usually his thing.

And yet… with those feathery tendrils of bright copper hair escaping from the top-knot on the crown of her head, and that cameo-carved profile turned towards him, he could be tempted to change his habits.

"So, your name isn't Smith after all," he remarked in a conversational tone. "Kirsty-Ann Tennison. Why did you choose not to use it?"

"You'd kidnapped me," she retorted caustically. "I didn't see why I should tell you my real name."

He laughed in genuine amusement. "What did you think I would do? Demand a ransom?"

She slanted him an icy glare, and turned her head away.

"Well, at least we're one step nearer the truth," he conceded. "Though it's like extracting teeth."

She continued to ignore him, her pretty chin tilted up at a haughty angle.

"Kirsty-Ann," he mused. "That's a nice name." He laughed at the expression of disgust which flickered across her face. "What's wrong with it?"

"Kirsty-Ann! Kirsty-Anns wear cutesy pink dresses and bows in their hair. That was the sort of daughter my mum wanted – instead she got me."

"You were a disappointment to her?"

"Well… no," she conceded. "Not exactly. But I think she would rather I hadn't been quite such a tomboy."

"So, am I to take it that you don't want me to call you Kirsty-Ann?" he enquired politely.

She slanted him a warning look. "Try it and I'll deck you again."

That made him laugh. "So what should I call you? And I very much doubt you could do it a second time," he added, deliberately taunting her.

"I'm Kat. And I certainly could."

"Kat - yes, that does suit you better," he acknowledged. "And for the record, the only reason you beat me the first time was because you caught me off guard."

"You think so?"

The challenge in those cool grey-green eyes hit him like a jolt of pure electricity. Yes, he could definitely be tempted to change his habits. "Why not put it to the test?" he suggested, injecting a provocative note of amusement into his voice. "A Randori – free sparring. First to three falls?"

Kat eyed him warily. It probably wouldn't be a good idea to risk any kind of physical contact with him. Not so much because she didn't trust him – somehow that very arrogance suggested that he was far too proud to resort to physical coercion.

But just being close to him was stirring odd little flutters in the pit of her stomach. Could she trust herself?

"Maybe some other time," she responded as casually as she could.

"You ought to give me a chance to redeem my pride," he argued reasonably. "If you win, I'll give you back your passport, and have Georges fly you wherever you want to go."

Kat hesitated. If he was willing to concede so much, he must be pretty confident of winning. But she'd competed against men his size before, who had also been confident. Too confident.

"And if you win…?" she queried.

"You're willing to concede that possibility?" he taunted.

"Not at all. You may be heavier and stronger than me, but that can be a positive disadvantage."

"It can indeed." He switched off the rower and rose easily to his feet.

"Now?" Her voice seemed to have risen an octave.

Those dark eyes mocked her cowardice. "When better?"

Her mouth was dry - and not just from her running. When he was standing so close beside her, she was far too aware of just how tall he was, the power of those hard muscles.

But as she had said, that wasn't necessarily to his advantage – it could be used against him. Possibly.

Struggling to steady her breathing, she nodded briskly. "OK – if you like."

That beguiling mouth curved into a slow, satisfied smile. Dammit, why had she let him lure her into agreeing to this?

For all her arguments against his size advantage, she had the very uncomfortable suspicion that this was going to prove to be a big mistake.

But she couldn't back out now.

Tilting up her chin, she followed him across the gym. Next to the squash court there was a large, airy space with a row of port-holes down one side, and competition-size judo mats laid out on the floor.

"There's kit in the cupboard."

"Th... Thank you."

Opening the door he indicated, she found a row of white double-weave cotton judogis of various sizes hanging on pegs. She chose one to fit her, and slipped it on over her shorts and T-shirt. Then she selected a black obi belt, wrapping it around her waist and tying it in a diamond knot.

"Ready?" He was tying his own belt – also black, she noted.

She drew in another deep breath. "Ready."

He smiled lazily. "Then let's go."

They walked to the middle of the mat, and bowed solemnly to each other. Kat eyed Javier warily as they took up their stance. Her aim was going to be to use the difference in their weight against him, to throw him off balance, but she knew he would be ready for her.

They paced in a circle for a good half minute, watching each other carefully, testing each other's responses, each alert for the other to try a sneaky manoeuver. Kat's breathing had settled now, her focus honed in on the task in hand, her mind empty of everything else.

Dancing on her toes, she tried a sharp reverse of direction, but Javier was with her, that dark gaze alert to her every move. He feinted to the left, but she out-guessed him, dodging out of his reach, managing to stay on her feet - but not quite quickly enough to transform it to her advantage.

He laughed softly. "You *are* good."

If he hoped his words would distract her enough that she wouldn't notice an attempted ankle hook, he quickly learned his mistake as she skipped aside, scooping an arm under his knee and swinging it swiftly up and back, grasping the lapel of his judogi jacket and using it to tip him over his own centre of gravity before he could do anything about it.

"Yes, I am," she agreed smartly as she stood over him in triumph.

She was acutely aware that there was a risk in goading him, but annoying him might make him careless.

Although maybe it had been too much of a risk, she acknowledged a few moments later when she found herself flat on her back on the mat, from a throw she hadn't even seen coming.

"All right," she conceded grudgingly. "All even."

They were both a little more circumspect now, learning to respect each other's skill. Both were breathing quite heavily, and Kat could feel a trickle of sweat running down her spine.

It was several minutes before either of them managed to outwit the other again. Kat was determined to show him that she was someone to be reckoned with. With all his money and power, he probably never had anyone stand up to him. If he didn't know already that she was different, he would find out.

That spirit seemed to give her an extra boost. Attuned to his slightest movement, she was swift to anticipate his next attack as he feinted a side-step. He twisted and caught her by the lapel, knocking her feet from under her and swinging her over his hip. But she rolled with the throw, landing on her feet instead of slamming to the floor.

Ducking under his arm to catch him while he was off balance, she tipped him clear over her back and skipped back in triumph as he landed on the mat.

Javier laughed, shaking his head to clear it. He was slightly winded, not just from landing hard on his back, but from finding himself there – again!

He had never fought a bout against a woman before, but he knew a few people who had, and they had told him that it wasn't something to take for granted. What they lacked in height, weight and sheer muscular strength they often made up in speed and subtlety.

So maybe he had underestimated her - it was something that wouldn't happen again. He had no intention of letting her have her passport and other possessions back until he knew what she had been doing here.

He stood up slowly. "Nice one," he approved.

"Are you OK?" she enquired – the flicker of amusement in her eyes warned him that she was asking less out of genuine concern for his well-being than from an entirely understandable desire to gloat.

"I'm fine. Shall we continue?"

"Ready when you are."

She was certainly quick – light on her feet, and never where he expected her to be. Just when he thought he had a grip on her, she was gone. Grappling close, she felt so delicate, but with an unmistakable core of strength, her body deceptively pliant, seeming to yield then retaliating with an attack he rarely anticipated. It was all he could do to hold his ground.

She would be this exciting in bed.

The thought of it ripped through him, a wave of heat that hit him square in the solar plexus. He had known from the first moment he had seen her, seen those long, lithe legs climbing the deck steps, what he wanted to do to her.

He wanted to get her naked, to taste every inch of that soft, silken skin, to feel that slender body wrapped around him, arching beneath him...

Kat was watching Javier warily as they circled each other again. He moved with the lithe grace of a jungle cat – a jungle cat stalking its prey.

When she had fought bouts against men before, she had only thought of them in terms of their martial arts skills. But this was different. Maybe it was the mocking glint in those dark eyes, but she was all too aware of him as a man.

A shimmer of heat ran through her. She had known there would be a risk in agreeing to this – being physically close to him, breathing the subtle, musky scent of his skin, matching her supple strength to his hard, muscular power... It was almost as if... they were making love...

But she couldn't let herself think like that, she reminded herself sharply. He would detect it, turn it to his advantage. *Focus...* She had to win this bout, win her freedom – get away from here and never see Javier de Almanzor again.

What had she been thinking, with her clever schemes to outwit him? She hated to let Amy down, but they would have to find another way. Maybe...

In that fleeting instant she had let herself be distracted, and found that Javier had twisted her abruptly off balance. She scrabbled for a grip on his jacket to keep her feet as she felt herself falling, but she was powerless to stop herself hitting the padded mat with a thud.

"Two all." Javier grinned as he held out his hand to help her to her feet. "Next fall decides the bout."

She returned him a grim smile, accepting his assistance to scramble to her feet only out of respect for the traditions of her sport, and disengaging as quickly as possible. To him this might be a game, but to her it was serious. Very serious.

Drawing in a deep, steadying breath she began circling around him again, watching him intently, ready for defense, planning her attack.

"Do you need a breather before we continue?" he enquired with a concern she had no trouble in dismissing as entirely spurious.

"No thank you. Do you?"

"Oh no - I'm enjoying myself. Very much." Those dark eyes were taunting her – he was deliberately trying to unsettle her, to distract her again. She wasn't going to let him.

They both feinted, on their toes, darting swiftly out of reach of any attack, probing for that split second advantage that would give one or other of them the edge.

Kat thought she had him when he went for a shoulder grip and she slipped aside, trying to snatch at his wrist and bring it back behind him, but he seemed to sense her move almost by instinct, recovering his balance as he twisted away from her.

Then he almost caught her with an unexpected two-fold attack to her left ankle and elbow. But it was a move very similar to one frequently used by one of her friends in New Zealand, and she ducked in beneath it, dropping to one knee and turning the move to her favour, using his weight to swing him over her shoulder.

But she hadn't put enough turn into the throw, and he landed on his feet. Using her momentum against her he tipped her off balance, toppling her backwards – she grabbed at his judogi to save herself, but it was too late. She crashed to the mat, as he came down on top of her, pinning her beneath him, both of them gasping for breath.

"Three!"

She couldn't quite accuse him of being smug, but there was a definite note of satisfaction in his voice as he claimed his victory.

He was still pinning her to the floor, his face just inches from hers, his eyes mesmerisingly dark as she gazed up into them. She was still breathing hard, and her mouth was so close to his that her parted lips felt like an invitation.

Summoning a spirit of defiance, she returned him a cool regard. "So? You didn't specify what your prize for winning would be."

"I didn't, did I?" A slow, mocking smile curved that sensuous mouth. "Now, what should I demand? Maybe… this…"

She knew she could resist – she knew she *should* resist. But her blood was already running hot with adrenalin, and her heightened awareness of his hard male body was luring her into abandoning her defenses.

His mouth met hers, warm and firm. His hot tongue slid along her lips, teasing into the corners, coaxing them apart, and the temptation to surrender chased all traces of rational thought from her mind.

She closed her eyes, losing herself in the sweet world of sensation that was surrounding her. His kiss was deep and tender, plundering all the deepest corners of her mouth.

The racing beat of her heart was pulsing her blood through her veins as if she had a fever, and her arms seemed to move of their own volition to wrap themselves around him as a deep sigh of pure pleasure shuddered through her.

His hands were stroking down over her body, caressing her slender curves. Her judogi jacket had fallen loose, and he smoothed it back, exposing long, slender column of her throat.

His hot mouth was tracing kisses down into the hollow of her shoulder, and a soft sigh escaped her lips as she felt the warmth of desire pool in the pit of her stomach…

Hell, what was she *doing*? This was Javier de Almanzor, the man who had seduced her innocent young step-sister and then coldly abandoned her when he had got her pregnant.

She was here to get revenge for that cruelty, not to fall for the same practiced trick herself.

He seemed to sense her sudden resistance, and drew back slightly, lifting himself on his elbow and arching one quizzical eyebrow. She took advantage of the moment, pushing against him and wriggling away, rolling over and rising quickly to her feet.

Laughing, he sat up, resting back on his hands. "You forgot to slap my face," he taunted. "Isn't that the usual conclusion of the 'Outraged Maiden' act?"

"Don't tempt me," she retorted hotly. "Do you usually hit on your crew?"

"Not usually," he conceded. "But then strictly speaking, you aren't crew."

"I could still sue you for sexual harassment."

"True - if you're willing to be dishonest enough to pretend you weren't kissing me back. With considerable enthusiasm, I might add."

Kat felt her cheeks flame a heated red. Much as she would have like to, she couldn't deny it – even to herself.

He laughed again, softly mocking. "Come on. It would have been naïve to think that wasn't inevitable from the moment I found you hiding behind my shirts. And don't believe either of us are naïve."

She turned on her heel and stalked away, stripping off her judogi as she went and tossing the pieces on the floor. As she slammed the gym door behind her, the last she heard of him was that mocking laughter.

## CHAPTER FIVE

"UGH – I hate early starts." Gill lifted her face from the pillow, and opened one eye. "You look all bright-eyed and bushy-tailed, as usual," she grumbled as Kat stepped through into the cabin from their small shared bathroom.

Kat laughed. "I'm used to early mornings," she responded breezily. "Besides, it'll make a change to have people aboard."

"Huh. You say that now. Just wait until you're running around after them, serving them drinks and cleaning up their rooms. '*Yes ma'am, no ma'am, three bags full ma'am.*' Spoiled bitches." She rolled out of the lower bunk, and grabbed her wash-bag. "Save me some breakfast."

After sailing south from Rome for a day or so, passing Sardinia and Sicily, they had turned east, heading out across Homer's wine-dark Ionian Sea. Now they had turned north, with the Greek mainland a low misty cloud on their port side as the sun rose, streaking the sky with pale magenta and gold like mother-of-pearl.

But Kat had little time to admire the view. It was a busy morning, preparing the saloons and staterooms for the guests who were due to come aboard that afternoon, polishing everything until it gleamed bright enough to satisfy even Maggie's critical eye. The Chief Stew checked every detail, making sure there were piles of fresh towels in each of the *en-suite* bathrooms, and no fluff under the beds.

It was a relief to sit down to lunch at the long table in the crew mess – today it was spicy pasta with jalapeno peppers. Kat tucked in with a hearty appetite, but the view out of the row of portholes was a distraction.

They had crossed the Gulf of Aegina during the morning, and now the low grey-green hills of the Greek coastline were sliding past on their starboard side. A rambling jumble of creamy-white buildings lined the coast and climbed the slopes behind – Athens, slumbering in the summer heat beneath an amber haze.

"OK people, let's get moving." The Second Officer rose to his feet and carried his plate over to the pot-wash. "We've got work to do."

Twenty minutes later Kat stood on deck with Gill to watch as they slipped smoothly into the Marina south of the city. The exclusive harbour was the epitome of luxury, the quayside paved with squares of terracotta blocks, and lined with high-end boutiques and lush flowerbeds.

There were several large yachts already moored there, but the Serenity was the largest – and to Kat's eye, the most beautiful.

The Captain steered her expertly into her berth against the outer boom, and before the deckhands had finished tying her up a truck had drawn up alongside, and vast quantities of fresh food supplies were soon being unloaded and stowed away in the chef's domain below decks.

Next to arrive was a van piled with expensive designer luggage. "Wow – how many people are we expecting?" Kat murmured to Gill as they watched a teetering pile of Vuitton suitcases being stacked onto a trolley and wheeled through the service hatch.

Gill laughed. "You ain't seen nothing yet! Come on, we need to make sure the right bags get to the right staterooms, and get them unpacked."

The guests arrived at around 3 o'clock. Three cars drew up on the quayside – a silver BMW, a long white limousine, and a hot red Ferrari with its roof down, which screeched to a stop with a jaunty blast on its horn.

The driver, a beautiful girl with a gleaming fall of black hair that reached half-way down her back and a well-rounded backside barely concealed by a tight yellow mini-dress, bounced out. She greeted Javier – who was standing by the rail – with an eager wave.

In her enthusiasm to run up the steps she apparently didn't notice Maggie, who was crossing the swim-deck with a pile of new bed-linen. She knocked it out of her hands, but just ignored it and darted up to where Javier was waiting, throwing her arms around his neck.

"Javier, *agape mou*!" she cried in delight, kissing him very determinedly on the lips.

"Who's that?" Kat asked Gill quietly.

Gill rolled her eyes. "That's Stasia – Stasia Dimitriou. She's a teeny bit crazy. She's determined to get her claws into Javier – she's got ambitions to be Senora de Almonzar. But that's never going to happen."

Kat's heart thumped. "You don't think so?"

Gill snorted with laughter. "Not likely! Apart from anything else, she's only eighteen – far too young for him."

Only a year younger than Amy, Kat reflected bitterly. But she made a conscious effort to keep her voice light. "He doesn't seem to mind her kissing him," she remarked.

"When did Javier ever mind a pretty girl kissing him?" Gill responded, laughing. "Let's face it, if flirting was an Olympic event, he'd clean up on every gold medal!"

Kat hoped the faint blush of pink that had risen to her cheeks wouldn't be noticed – or that if it was, it would be ascribed to her exertions unpacking the suitcases and hanging all the fabulous designer clothes in the wardrobes.

Accustomed to travelling light herself, she had been stunned by the amount of stuff someone might consider necessary for what she had been told would be a cruise of only a couple of weeks.

"Mind you, it wouldn't have been a surprise if he had married that one," Gill added as an elegant blonde beauty in a white trouser-suit climbed out of the BMW.

"Who is she?" Kat frowned slightly – the woman looked faintly familiar.

"Celine. The face that launched a million lipsticks. You can't have missed her unless you've been hiding under a rock these past five years – she's been all over the billboards and magazines. She used to date Javier a couple of years ago, but she dumped him – or more likely he dumped her. She's married to Stasia's brother Jasen now. That's him."

A tall man, film-star handsome but with a petulant set to his mouth, followed his wife as she sashayed onto the yacht. She greeted Javier with a cool peck on the cheek – though the look she slanted at him would have ignited asbestos.

"And that's their father, with his latest trophy wife," added Gill as an older man and a stunning dark-haired creature, all lush curves poured into a crimson dress, emerged languidly from the limousine. "Talia Petrakis. She used to be some kind of TV star in Greece, before she married Fedor. I'm not sure if she's wife number four or number five – I've lost count." She chuckled with laughter. "This could be an entertaining voyage."

It certainly could, Kat mused as she watched the three women circle around Javier like bees around a honey-pot. But she wasn't sure if she was going to enjoy it.

Javier disentangled himself gently but firmly from Stasia's grip, and smiled in welcome as Fedor Dimitriou came up the steps from the swim-deck.

"Fedor - good to see you," he greeted him in the man's native tongue, shaking his hand. "How have you been keeping?"

"Pretty well," the older man acknowledged genially. "Looking forward to a nice sea cruise – and a little bit of business."

Javier smiled. "I think I can promise you both," he responded. "But for now, come and have a drink."

"Ah – an excellent suggestion. Talia, my dear," he added, turning to his wife, "would you care for a drink now, or would you prefer to be shown to our cabin?"

"Of course I'll have a drink, darling." She took her husband's arm, but her eyes slid to Javier's, and he couldn't miss the message they conveyed.

The smile he returned was tight and cynical. It was going to be an interesting trip, but he wasn't sure if he was going to enjoy it.

They had moved onto the aft-deck, where a green-and-white striped canopy provided some shelter from the hot Greek sun. A couple of the stewardesses were there, waiting discreetly to serve them with drinks and canapés – with a quick glance Javier confirmed the presence of one stewardess in particular.

He knew that Maggie, his Chief Stew, expected the crew to be as invisible as possible, but there was no way Kat Tennison could ever be invisible, not with that gleaming copper hair, again tied in a knot on the top of her head.

The crew Number Ones - a mannish white shirt with dark green epaulettes and ribbon tie, and dark green culottes - had never looked better than on that slender but undeniably feminine shape. Somehow she made it look as elegant as any of the expensive designer outfits his female guests were wearing.

She stood with a quiet but far from servile patience while Stasia jabbered on about a new bikini she had bought, wondering whether it was just a little too risqué, slanting him an overtly flirtatious glance as she speculated on whether the top would stay on if she swam in it, seemingly oblivious to her father's warning frown.

"So, Fedor, what would you like to drink?" he intervened before father and daughter could launch into one of their spectacular spats.

"I'll have a whisky and soda."

Stasia ordered a Tequila Slammer, Celine and Talia opted for vodka martinis, and Jasen for a gin and tonic.

"And I'll have my usual," he said.

Those silk-fringed grey-green eyes turned to him. "And that is…?

Her voice was cool with indifference - but he wasn't fooled. A slight flush of pink had coloured her cheeks – she was remembering, as he was, their encounter in the gym. Remembering how their close-fought battle had ended in the sweetest surrender, and a kiss so sizzlingly hot it had lingered into his dreams.

"Mineral water – still, not sparkling - with a slice of lime."

She bent her head in the briefest nod of acknowledgement, then turned away. He watched as she crossed the saloon to the bar, lithe and slender, that neat derrière swaying slightly as she walked.

It would be very pleasant to remove each item of that formal uniform, he mused – slowly, very slowly, to discover the smooth, silky skin beneath…

"Javier, did you get that new jet-ski?" Stasia's intrusive demand sliced through his wayward thoughts. "I'm dying to try it out. You haven't let anyone else use it yet, have you? You promised me I could be first."

Kat gritted her teeth as she carried the drinks across the room on a silver tray and handed them out. Not one single word of thanks was forthcoming – except from Javier, who caught her eye with a wicked smile which almost startled her into dropping his drink.

But of course he probably found this amusing, making her wait on his glamorous guests.

She couldn't understand the conversation – they were speaking what she presumed must be Greek – but she had no difficulty interpreting the body-language. The younger one, whom Gill had said was called Stasia, was pouting prettily at Javier, commandeering his attention – it might be wishful thinking, but she sensed that he was treating her as he might one of his nieces, with a kind of avuncular indulgence that showed no sexual interest whatsoever.

The blonde had arranged herself with studied super-model elegance on one of the loungers. "Oh, do please speak English," she protested, pouting those famous bee-stung lips. "Or at least French. You know I don't speak a word of Greek."

"I'm sorry, my dear," Fedor responded, smiling. "We will try to remember."

Talia's fine dark eyes rolled to express her opinion, and she slanted an amused look towards Javier, clearly inviting him to agree with her.

*Oh great*, Kat reflected with a touch of asperity. *A dysfunctional family – that's all we need.*

So he had dated Celine? That was little surprise – she really was exceptionally beautiful, with cheekbones to die for, and that gleaming tumble of just-got-out-of-bed golden blonde hair.

Who had been the dumper and who the dumpee? she wondered. The way Celine was looking at Javier, with those come-hither eyes, suggested that she was still more than interested – apparently disregarding the fact that her husband of less than a year was sitting just a few feet away.

But after all, why should she care if Javier chose to rekindle their affair? It was nothing to do with her. She had known when he had kissed her that it didn't mean a thing to him.

And it hadn't meant a thing to her either, so she certainly wasn't *jealous*. She was just… angry on poor Amy's account, that she had been cheated by such an unrepentant rake.

Of course that kiss had meant nothing. As Gill had said, he was pretty indiscriminate with his kisses. She had to remember that, to armour herself against the memory that had been so vivid it had lingered into her dreams…

♥

They sailed in the late afternoon. By the time they had finished serving the guests a leisurely dinner, followed by after-dinner drinks in front of the giant plasma TV screen where they had watched the Formula One Grand Prix until the small hours of the morning, Kat's feet were aching and she was feeling exhausted.

But she couldn't sleep. The images and events of the evening kept playing through her mind as she analysed every detail of Javier's interactions with the three Greek women, searching for any sign that he might be interested in any of them.

And though she was furious with herself for letting her mind dwell on him so obsessively, she couldn't stop herself dissecting every brief glance in her direction, the way he had sometimes seemed to be watching her as she had moved around the dinner table, the enigmatic smiles he had slanted towards her from time to time.

He had made her feel as if there was some secret connection between them, an invisible gossamer thread. Was that how he operated, keeping three or four women stringing along by making each one think she was the special one?

Trying to fidget quietly so as not to waken Gill was giving her cramp. Eventually she slipped out of her bunk, pulled on her shorts and T-shirt and a warm green fleece jacket that went with the crew uniform. Then she slipped out of the cabin, and up the steps to the aft deck.

It was a beautiful night. There was no moon; the sea was like black silk, seamed by the white lacy froth of their wake, the sky was inky velvet spangled with a million stars. She had never seen so many stars, the lofty sweep of the milky-way curving down to the far horizon, invisible in the darkness.

She leaned against the rail, gazing out at the sky. The cool night breeze tugged at her hair, the only sound was the soft swish of the waves rushing beneath the white hull. There was no land in sight, no other boats. With only their running-lights showing, they were all alone on the vast empty expanse of water.

It was as if they were chasing the stars through the night…

"If you were planning to swim to the shore, I should warn you that it's over twenty miles." A voice spoke, laced with sardonic amusement. "And it's that way."

She turned sharply as Javier strolled down the steps from the upper deck, a dark glint of amusement in his eyes as he pointed in the opposite direction from where she was standing.

"Or were you just having trouble sleeping?" he taunted softly. "I must admit, I was too. My bed is very comfortable, but it can feel a bit too large with just me in it."

"I wouldn't have thought you'd have a problem arranging to have company," she returned, mentally kicking herself for the trace of bitterness in her voice – he was going to think she was jealous.

He laughed – a low, husky sound that did dangerous things to her pulse-rate. "But I am. You turned me down, remember?"

"I… didn't mean me," she countered stiffly.

"But of my guests, two are married – and I don't sleep with married women – and the other is far too young and far too much of a chatterbox."

"I didn't think you'd be so picky." She let a deliberate note of contempt slip into her voice.

"Ah – alas for my playboy reputation." He sighed theatrically. "I've had far fewer affairs than the gossip magazines would have you believe, you know."

"It's really no concern of mine," she retorted. She turned her back on him, but she was still far too conscious of him, standing far too close behind her.

"It's a beautiful night," he remarked. "Were you watching the stars?"

"Yes." She really didn't want to speak to him, but she knew he wasn't going to go away. "There's a lot more out here than you usually see."

"That's because there are no city lights to dim them out. Do you see those four stars that make a large square? That's

Pegasus." He pointed over her shoulder, and she was able to pick out the distinctive square of bright stars. "Now move your eye up and a little to the left. See that kind of blurred oval shape? That's the Andromeda Galaxy. It's the most distant object that can be seen with the naked eye – it's about two and a half million light years away."

She slanted him a look of surprise. "You're interested in astronomy?"

"Sailors are always interested in the stars."

"I'd have thought you'd have all sorts of instruments on a boat like this to find your way."

"Of course. But it's wise not to always rely on them." His smile was enigmatic. "If in doubt, you should always follow your star."

He turned her to face him, and she found that she didn't have the strength to resist. With one finger he stroked down over her cheek, a touch as light as a butterfly's wing; then over the soft fullness of her lips, and then down beneath her chin to tilt her face up to his.

Something seemed to have stopped her breathing. His mouth was barely an inch from hers, and she found herself remembering the way he had kissed her before. The soft night breeze was whispering around her, sweet siren songs that tempted her to surrender – *kiss him… kiss him…*

She put up her hands against the solid wall of his chest, telling herself that she intended to push him away, but as her fingertips encountered the hard resilience of male muscle beneath his warm skin she felt her resistance crumbling.

Did she sway towards him first, or did he lower his head to hers…? It didn't matter. Nothing mattered but this moment, as the ache of need inside her dissolved into molten gold, melting her bones.

His sensuous tongue swirled over the sensitive membranes inside her lips, sending hot little shivers of pleasure scudding down her spine. She was responding mindlessly, her supple body curved against his as his arms folded around her, drawing her close.

With every breath his subtle musky male scent was filling her senses, sweetly intoxicating. The warm night breeze drifting across the inky sea seemed to wrap around them like a velvet cloak.

Kat felt so light that a whisper of starlight could have wafted her away. Only Javier was real, solid. And he was the only thing she wanted...

He lifted his head, a dark glint of satisfaction in those mesmerising gold-flecked eyes as they gazed down into hers. "So, where does your star lead?" he asked softly.

Kat stared up at him, reality hitting her like a splash of cold water. How could she let herself be so stupid, so weak? This was the one man above all others she shouldn't touch with a very long pole. She *knew* that, so why did she seem unable to remember it?

She eased herself out of his grip, edging along the rail. "Away from you," she asserted, raw determination in her voice.

That beguiling mouth curved into a sardonic smile. "Are you sure?"

"Very sure."

He didn't try to stop her as she walked away. "If you change your mind..."

She slanted him a withering glance over her shoulder. "Do please hold your breath while you're waiting," she retorted.

He laughed out loud. "Ah, that's a good one," he approved. "That's a very good one."

♥ ♥ ♥

"Yes Ma'am, no ma'am, three bags full ma'am."

"Told you so," Gill returned quietly, slotting pieces of marinated chicken, bacon and mushrooms onto a wooden skewer. "If Stasia eats any more of these kebabs she's going to bust out of that bikini."

"She's eating Celine's share," Kat muttered, stooping to load the empty glasses she had collected into the dishwasher behind the swim-up bar. "I swear all that woman had for lunch was half a lentil lightly grilled in fairy spit."

Gill supressed a giggle. "Shhh – Maggie'll bust a gasket if she catches us laughing at the guests."

"It's better than what I'd like to do to them. Picking up after them morning, noon and night, waiting on them hand and foot – well, OK. But never so much as a whisper of a thank you. They look through you as if you aren't even there." She laughed wryly, straightening her back. "Oh, I'm sorry for grumbling. I just need to let off steam."

"No need to apologise - they drive me crazy too. I don't know which is worse – Fedor's lot or the Russians."

"Hmmm." Kat slanted a jaded glance around the swimming pool. "Hard to choose between them."

They had passed through the Dardanelles on Tuesday morning, and arrived on the eastern shore of the Black Sea a day later, anchoring in a sheltered bay close to a town called Novorossiysk, a sprawling industrial conurbation on the Russian coast.

A clutch of hatchet-faced Russian businessmen had come aboard that afternoon, accompanied by their glamorous wives and girlfriends, and a phalanx of bodyguards all built like ten-ton trucks and refusing to take off the jackets of their formal dark grey suits, which seemed to be a kind of uniform.

While the men were closeted with Javier and Fedor, and sometimes Jasen, up in his office on the bridge deck, their women were engaged in a contest with the Dimitriou women to wear the teeniest bikini, to lounge the most languidly in the hot afternoon sun.

In spite of its rather forbidding name, the Black Sea was really rather beautiful – tranquil and blue beneath a cloudless sky, with a pleasantly cool breeze just ruffling the green-and-white awning over the aft-deck.

But she had had little time to enjoy it. The crew had been rushed off their feet, running around after the guests - serving meals, fetching drinks, making beds, keeping the whole yacht in the pristine condition Maggie demanded.

Nor had she seen much of Javier, apart from at dinner each evening, and sometimes later if she had been on the late shift to serve drinks and snacks in the cinema or around the pool. Which suited her just fine. The less she saw of him the better.

"Got any more lemons?" Gill asked, checking over the ingredients for the vinaigrette.

"Yes – there's a couple in the fridge…" Suddenly a shadow fell across her, and she glanced up to find one of the bodyguards had approached the bar from the dry side. "You have beer?" he enquired.

"Certainly." She reached into the chill shelf for a bottle of premium lager. But as she handed it to him, his giant fist closed over hers, gripping tightly.

"You be nice to me?" he leered, pulling her towards him over the bar.

Her instinctive reaction was a breakaway move, but even as she rethought whether it was necessary in this situation a voice of cool amusement spoke behind her.

"I really wouldn't do that if I were you." Javier's dark eyes fixed steadily on the gorilla. "I mean it – she can be very dangerous."

The guy glared back at him for a moment, then appeared to realise who had confronted him. With what could be taken as a muttered word of apology in Russian, he took his beer and retreated to the far side of the pool.

"Has he been bothering you?" Javier asked.

"Nothing I couldn't handle."

"That's not the point. You… My crew shouldn't be subjected to that kind of harassment."

He smiled down at her, and somehow she couldn't stop herself smiling back. And there it was again, that strange sense of connection, for just a few seconds...

Then Fedor and Jasen and the Russian businessmen came up to the bar, talking and laughing loudly, apparently in jovial spirits. Kat turned away from Javier to take their drink orders, doing her best to ignore the sensation that he was still watching her.

After a moment he strolled away with the others to take their places on the sun loungers around the pool. Jackets came off, shirt collars were loosened, cuffs rolled back. The female contingent, moments before as somnolent as cats, suddenly stirred, all fluttering eyelashes and flirtatious smiles.

"Let battle commence," murmured Kat.

It was apparent that with their business concluded it was time to play. As the vodka flowed, the party grew rowdier. Some of the men – including some of the Russian bodyguards – had gone off to change into swimming trunks, and soon the pool was filled with bodies of all shapes and sizes.

A ball appeared from somewhere, and a noisy game of water polo was begun – not that it appeared to follow any known rules of the game. Some of the women were on the men's shoulders – Stasia had chosen a particularly beefy bodyguard and was flirting outrageously with him, while regularly checking whether Javier was noticing.

Kat, on the other hand, was trying very hard to resist the temptation to check if he was looking in her direction. She had enough to do, collecting up glasses and plates, serving drinks, fetching more towels and adjusting sunshades in response to the imperious demands of his guests.

She had her hands full with a tray of empty glasses when Stasia chose to launch herself from her swain's shoulders into a spectacular backward flop, tossing up a mini-tsunami of water which splashed over her, soaking her hair and her white shirt.

Of course there was no apology – the girl didn't even seem to notice, far too busy laughing and teasing the unfortunate bodyguard, who was looking as if he had just received an unexpected birthday gift and wasn't sure if it was going to explode in his hands.

Javier swam up to the edge of the pool, resting his arms on the side. "You're wet," he remarked. "You'd better go and change."

"No, it's fine," she insisted. "It'll dry off in a few minutes."

He smiled that lazily sardonic smile. "Do you disagree with me just for the sake of being contrary?" he enquired.

"No." She stooped to pick up a glass which had fallen from the tray. "I just disagree with you."

"You did it again."

"What?"

"Disagreed with me."

She was forced to return his smile, shaking her head.

"Now you're supposed to say, 'No I didn't,'" he teased.

Her eyes sparkled with amusement. "But I did."

"Is this the five minute argument, or the thirty minute argument?"

She gurgled with laughter. "Do you always quote Monty Python when…"

They were interrupted by Stasia, swimming up behind Javier and wrapping her arms tightly around his neck. "Come on Javier, don't be a bore," she begged, slanting an acid glare towards Kat. "We need you on our team."

He gently unfolded her arms. "I'll be there in a moment."

"No, now," she pouted insistently. "We're losing."

Kat turned her back and walked away.

## CHAPTER SIX

JAVIER leaned back in his big leather office chair, and propped his bare feet up on the edge of the desk, easing the kinks out of his wide shoulders. It had been a good week, business-wise. He and Fedor had successfully negotiated a string of contracts relating to the shipping of wheat, metals and oil with the Russians, worth a good few million.

Now they were back on the western shore of the Black Sea, awaiting clearance from the traffic controller to proceed into the narrow Bosporus strait. His Captain had timed it well, as usual – it was early afternoon, and the flow of ships coming north had cleared a short time ago, allowing the south-bound vessels to take their turn.

A couple of large container ships were ahead of them, but with the current in their favour on this run, even at a stately six knots it would only take a couple of hours to get through.

Idly he leaned over and switched the computer to the on-board CCTV channel. His guests were all lounging beside the pool. Jasen and Fedor seemed to be having a mild argument – that was nothing unusual. Jasen wanted his father to give him more responsibility in the family business, but Fedor – with some justification – didn't regard him as competent.

This trip had been partly a test of that, but unfortunately Jasen had shown more interest in trying out the yacht's jet-skis and mini-sub than discussing tanker capacity – though he may have been more keen to get involved if Fedor hadn't relegated him to the role of gofer during the negotiations.

And then there were the women of the family.

Stasia was wearing that famous bikini – the strapless twist of fluorescent yellow across her ample bosom didn't really do her any favours, though fortunately it hadn't actually fallen off yet. Celine was wearing even less – lying on her stomach with her white bikini top discarded beside her, and only a thong to preserve whatever modesty she might still claim. Talia, as usual, was asleep in the shade. She was like a cat, that woman – she seemed to sleep all the time, when she wasn't eating.

Quickly he scanned through the other images. Several of the crew who were off-duty were swimming off the swim-steps on the starboard side...

He wasn't specifically looking for her, of course. But there was no denying she looked pretty damn good in a plain dark blue swimsuit, wet and clinging to every delicious inch of her as she hauled herself up out of the water and squeezed the droplets of water from the long hank of copper curls hanging over her shoulder.

And then... she hooked her fingers into the bottom of her swimsuit and ran them round over the smooth curve of her backside to ease the fabric back into place. Something hit him right in the solar plexus. It was a totally unconscious action, totally innocent and yet compellingly sensual.

He watched as she skipped nimbly up the swim-steps. Someone called out to her, and she turned back, laughing – he couldn't hear her, only see, of course, but he knew the sound of that laughter. He had heard it frequently around the boat this past couple of weeks – a rippling, melodic sound that made you want to laugh with her.

And everyone did. His whole crew, from the Captain down, seemed to be captivated by her. She had Fedor chuckling as if he was her uncle, Jasen trying to flirt with her – even Talia had opened those feline eyes long enough to be gracious. The only one who seemed petulantly resistant to her charm was Stasia, of course.

But he never got the chance to laugh with her himself.

It was quite an achievement that she seemed able to avoid him within the confines of a boat not much bigger than a football pitch. But apart from mealtimes, when her duties required her to help serve at table, all he seemed to see of her was a flash of that bright copper head disappearing around a corner, a pair of long, slender legs dancing up a flight of stairs.

He watched as she walked back to the crew quarters, moving from screen to screen across the CCTV, a towel slung around her shoulders, somehow managing to walk elegantly in flip-flops…

"Got a minute, boss?"

Javier flicked off the TV screen, but the look on the face of his chief of security told him he hadn't been quite quick enough. "Yes Bob – what is it?" he asked as blandly as he could.

"I've got the checks on Antipov. It all looks above board. He's done a fair amount of business with Voronin over the past ten years or so."

Javier nodded, holding out his hand for the buff folder Bob was holding. "That's as good a recommendation as I'd look for. Anything on Yermalov?"

"Clean so far. I've a few more leads to check out."

"Good work. Thank you."

"What about the girl?"

Javier glanced up at him, wavering between an innocent, 'What girl?' and biting his security chief's head off. Instead he sighed. "Yes, I know. I should have handed her over to the police right away, I should have put her ashore in Athens."

Bob laughed. "Well, yes – that would have been the sensible thing to do. But to be honest, I see no harm in her. I've been watching her pretty close, and so far she hasn't put a foot wrong. She's either very clever, or she's kosher."

"Still nothing on a police record?"

"Nothing. Not the UK or Europe, Canada, Singapore, Australia or New Zealand. The US is going to take a little longer, and I've got someone in Hong Kong to take a look."

"So – she is who she appears to be?"

"If you don't ask what she was doing stowing away."

"Looking for adventure?" Javier suggested lightly.

"From what I've found out, she's had plenty of that," Bob remarked with a grin. "Trekking in Nepal, running safaris in Tanzania, white water rafting in New Zealand…"

"She gets around." Javier opened a drawer in his desk and pulled out her passport. The pages were covered in visa and entry/exit stamps from all over the world.

Idly he flipped through them, then turned to the front to look at her photograph again. Somehow even in that regimented, unsmiling image she radiated a kind of sparkle, those wide grey-green eyes alive with warmth and humour.

Bob glanced down at the picture. "She's a looker alright," he accorded. "And in spite of everything, she seems like a nice kid."

Javier arched one dark eyebrow in wry amusement. "You too, Bob?"

"What?" Bob grinned, uncharacteristically sheepish. "Well, yeah. But I still think you should have put her ashore."

"You could be right," Javier conceded. But he wasn't sorry he had kept her aboard. Even if she was treating him as if he had some kind of contagious disease.

♥ ♥ ♥

"Thanks for swapping shifts with me, Kat." Gill wriggled herself into a bright pink body-con dress that looked fabulous on her, and shook out her hair. "Are you sure you don't want to go ashore?"

"No, you go ahead," Kat assured her, smiling. "I'm fine."

"Well, if you're sure…"

They had docked in the old harbour of Mykonos an hour ago, and most of the crew were taking the opportunity to spend an evening ashore. One of the girls was celebrating her birthday, and it was likely to be quite a wild night.

That had been Kat's excuse to say that she was happy to let Gill go and party with her friends, avoiding the need to explain why she didn't have her passport.

There would be little to do anyway. The Dimitrious had also gone ashore for dinner, the three women glamorous in designer dresses, dripping with jewellery. Kat hadn't seen whether Javier had gone with them, and she certainly wasn't going to ask.

She served dinner for the First Mate and the Chief Engineer, set the table in the crew-mess for breakfast, topped up all the condiments in the pantry and polished the silverware. With everything finished, she had just sat down to watch television for a few minutes when the Sous-Chef stuck his head round the door.

"Coffee for Javier, Kat. Up in the Skylounge."

She looked up sharply. "I thought he'd gone ashore?"

He shook his head. "You'll find everything you need up there in the pantry. He likes it strong, with a dash of cream and no sugar."

She pulled a face as she rose to her feet. "You'd think he could manage to make himself a cup of coffee," she remarked acidly.

"He usually does. He must be working tonight."

Drawing in a long, deep breath, Kat checked that she was looking presentable – she had taken off her green ribbon-tie some time ago, but her shirt still looked white and crisp.

Damn the man, she cursed to herself as she rode the service lift to the upper deck. Shouldn't he be entertaining his guests ashore? If it wasn't such a ludicrous idea, she might almost have suspected him of doing this deliberately.

Since the night he had kissed her, she had been doing her best to avoid him. It hadn't been easy – particularly as she had had to serve at the tables at mealtimes. It had taken a lot of willpower to avoid glancing in his direction, particularly when sometimes she had felt a kind of tingle on the back of her neck, as if he was watching her.

And that kiss was still vivid in her mind, though it was more than two weeks ago now. Her lips felt warm just thinking about it. She wasn't sure why he'd done it – probably just because he could. No doubt he was accustomed to women welcoming his kisses, his caresses, however casually bestowed.

The lift doors opened and she stepped out into the small lobby, and tapped on the door to the lounge. A familiar voice called, "Come in."

Javier was sprawled on a leather sofa, watching Formula One motor racing on a giant plasma-screen television. So much for working so hard he couldn't make his own coffee, Kat reflected tartly.

He barely turned his head as she entered, merely flickering a sardonic glance towards her, acknowledging her presence with a brief nod of his head.

She tilted up her chin at a haughty angle, and retreated quickly to the small pantry.

There was a high-tech coffee machine on the counter, and she busied herself tipping a scoop of beans into the filter and filling the tank with water, hoping her back conveyed her total disinterest as eloquently as possible.

"Why don't you make one for yourself, and join me?"

He stood in the doorway, leaning one wide shoulder against the frame. Kat licked a random splash of cream from her thumb before answering coolly, "No thank you."

"Still avoiding me?" he taunted softly

"Is this how you choose to amuse yourself?" she countered. "Hitting on your crew?"

He tipped head on one side as if considering her accusation. "Well, technically speaking you aren't crew," he argued. "You're a stowaway working her passage – that's quite a different thing. And would you call it 'hitting on' you? I would tend to define 'hitting on' as inflicting unwelcome attention. But I really don't think you can claim in all honesty that my attentions have been unwelcome. Could you?"

Those dark eyes caught hers, holding them in their mesmerising gaze. Kat felt a blush of pink rise to her cheeks – no, she couldn't claim that his kisses had been unwelcome, much as she would have wanted to.

But this was the man who had ruthlessly seduced poor Amy – she wasn't going to let the same thing happen to her.

On the other hand, she reasoned to herself, this voyage would soon be over. If she continued to maintain too much distance between them she would run out of opportunities to find the evidence she was looking for. It was a risk, but perhaps one worth taking.

So long as she was careful, didn't let him get too close… and kept her own treacherous reaction to him strictly under control…

He recognised her slight hesitation, and was quick to layer on the persuasive charm. "After all, you have to admit it's much nicer up here than down in the crew mess," he coaxed. "Besides, I would enjoy your company."

"Oh really?" A deliberate note of sarcasm edged her voice. "Poor little rich boy, all alone. Why didn't you go ashore with your guests?"

He laughed dryly. "Don't you think I deserve a break from work?"

"You call squiring a Greek princess to a nightclub work?"

"When the Greek princess in question is Stasia Dimitriou, yes I do," he asserted.

Kat arched one finely-drawn eyebrow in polite scepticism.

"She's very pretty, but that incessant chatter does my head in." He turned on that beguiling smile. "Come on, sit down. I'm suggesting conversation – I'm not planning to make love to you."

"I'm pleased to hear it. But please, don't let me interrupt your viewing."

"It's only the qualifying rounds," he remarked dismissively. "The grid is pretty much settled – I don't expect any big surprises now." He picked up the remote and turned the television off.

Instead of sitting down, she wandered over to the window, holding her coffee-mug. The Skylounge was well-named – situated for'ard on the very top deck of the yacht, it was almost entirely clad in glass, with a glass ceiling. When the boat was in motion it almost felt as if you were flying.

Tonight the view was of the sweeping curve of the bay, the dark water shimmering with golden reflections of the lights along the crowded harbour front. Above the harbour the lights traced the jumble of streets rising up the gentle slopes of the surrounding hills, and picked out the distinctive row of pepper-pot windmills against the night sky.

"It is an amazing view," she acknowledged.

"Have you ever been to Mykanos before?"

"I came here a couple of years ago, with some friends. We weren't allowed to dock in the Old Harbour."

"They don't let sailing boats in anymore," he explained. "It's been like that for… oh, twenty years or so."

"But billionaires with over-sized yachts are welcome?"

He put on a hurt look. "Would you call her over-sized?" he protested.

"Well… No." She conceded a smile. "She's beautiful. How long have you had her?"

"I bought her four years ago. I had a smaller one before – just eighty metres."

"Oh, poor you. How pokey! No wonder you needed a bigger one."

He shook his head. "Oh, she's not just a private pleasure palace - she's an integral part of my business. It isn't just about the space, it's about the image. She needs to impress."

"Well, she certainly does that. So, that's what you do, is it? A kind of glorified taxi-driver?"

He laughed, a rich velvet sound. "It's not quite as simple as that."

"Oh?"

"My business is brokerage – commodities brokerage. Let us say that Mr A has something which he wishes to transport, and Mr B has a fleet of cargo ships which he would like to fill. But Mr B lives in Athens and speaks no Russian, while Mr A lives in Russia and speaks no Greek. They may be interested in doing business together, if they could only meet."

"So you arrange for them to meet?"

"Exactly," he concurred. "But then they do not understand each other's language. Each needs to have an interpreter whom they can trust, someone who understands the laws of international commerce. When there are millions, maybe even billions of dollars involved, that may not be easy to arrange. They are understandably wary."

"Which is where you come in."

He nodded. "I speak both Russian and Greek, I know each of them, I know how they like to do business. They trust me. So, they meet here on my yacht – neutral territory for both of them. And they are willing to pay me a good commission for acting as an intermediary for them. And everyone is happy."

"So it's not all sunshine and swimming pools?"

He laughed again, his head thrown back. "You know, you're a very refreshing experience," he remarked. "I don't recall that I ever met a woman with such an acerbic tongue."

"Then the circles you're mixing in are too restricted," she countered. "It's not good for you, having people sucking up to you all the time – it over-inflates your ego. I suppose that's the penalty of being filthy rich."

He sighed in mock regret. "You could be right. I'm very fortunate to have encountered you."

"I'm glad you recognise it." She found herself laughing with him. Dangerous, she warned herself sternly – don't let yourself start liking him.

She strolled casually around the lounge. It was furnished with comfortable-looking sofas of cream-coloured hide, but she was too antsy to sit down - though not quite yet willing to leave.

"So, do you spend a lot of your time aboard, apart from when you're doing your brokering?"

"As much as I can," he responded, lounging back easily in his seat and crossing one ankle over the other knee. "It's very peaceful – no crowds, no traffic."

"Don't you get bored?"

"Rarely. If I feel the desire for company, I can always invite guests aboard, or choose to go ashore wherever the fancy takes me."

"Do you have a house on land?" she asked innocently, as if she had never heard of Google.

"I have several," he acknowledged. "An apartment in Barcelona, one in London and another in New York. And a ski-lodge in the French Alps. But I tend to feel cooped up if I spend too long in any of them."

Kat stiffened at the mention of the ski-lodge – but fortunately she was behind him, so he couldn't have noticed. She continued to stroll around the room, struggling to keep her heartbeat steady.

"What about your family?" she asked, careful to keep only a note of polite interest in her voice.

"Oh, they're happy enough for me to keep my visits home to a minimum," he responded, laughing. "It avoids too many arguments with my father."

"You don't get on?"

He tipped his head on one side, watching her with idle curiosity - as if wondering at her curiosity about him. "Generally we get along pretty well," he conceded. "There's really only one bone of contention. He thinks I should stay home and help manage the family estates - I think my brother is more than capable of managing without me getting under his feet. It's something we've disagreed on since I was seventeen. My mother says we're too much alike. Both obstinate and opinionated."

Kat laughed. "She sounds like a very perceptive woman."

"She's very wise," he agreed. "Are you going to continue to pace around like a cat in a cage, or are you going to come and sit down and have a cup of coffee?"

She hesitated, then moved over casually to sit on the sofa opposite him. "Do you have any other brothers and sisters?" she asked, sipping her coffee.

That smile flickered across his face, a hint of sardonic amusement. "Just one sister - she's the eldest. And a crop of nieces and nephews, and more cousins than I could count. That's probably why I like to escape to sea whenever I can."

"So what else do you do, when you're not cruising?" This was the point to be cautious. She had chosen not to jump on his remark about the ski-lodge immediately, to avoid arousing his suspicion – it was better to track towards it in a roundabout way.

"Oh, just the usual sort of thing." Another shrug of those wide shoulders. "When I'm in London or New York I might go to the theatre, when I'm in Australia I'll go diving. And if I can catch up with the Formula One circuit at the right time I'll go and watch a race."

"And skiing?" she suggested carefully.

"If I can get away at the right time of the season."

There was no perceptible constraint in his manner. If he even remembered the innocent young girl he had seduced and ruthlessly dumped on his last skiing trip, he appeared to harbour not a shred of guilt.

"So, your turn." Those dark eyes regarded her levelly across the space between them. "Oh, I've no intention of trying to pry into your secrets – I'm quite sure you would only give me more lies. But there must be some things that wouldn't breach the Official Secrets Act. For example, when did you take up Krav Maga?"

She hesitated, but there could be little harm in telling him about that. "A few years ago," she conceded. "I've been doing judo since I was twelve. I was being bullied at school because of my dyslexia, and my step-father thought it would give me confidence."

"And did it?"

She laughed dryly. "Funnily enough, as soon as the other kids found out I was doing martial arts, I didn't have any more trouble. After that, it was just the teachers."

"Oh?" He appeared genuinely interested, and she found herself continuing.

"Not many of them knew how to deal with my dyslexia. Some of them didn't even believe it existed – they said I was just lazy. So my step-father sent me to a different school, which was brilliant."

"Sounds like he's a good step-father."

She hesitated for a fraction of a breath – she had to be careful not to give too much away. "He is," she concurred, memories making her smile.

"And will your family be wondering where you are?"

"It's a little late to be showing concern about that," she retorted.

He laughed dryly. "Since you seemed to be showing no concern yourself, I assumed not."

She shrugged her slender shoulders. "Well… No they won't worry. I'm often out of contact when I'm travelling."

"You travel a lot?"

"A fair amount." She began to let herself relax a bit - it had been a long day, and she was a little sleepy. And the sofa was *very* comfortable. "Like you, I get bored if I'm cooped up for too long."

He smiled, what seemed to be a genuine smile, lighting his eyes. "Welcome to a fellow gypsy," he accorded.

"Mind you, I don't usually travel in anything like this kind of style," she added, her glance encompassing the elegant lounge. "It's usually a back-pack and a bouncy old Land Rover."

He laughed. "Yes, I saw from your passport that you've been to some fairly exotic places."

The mention of her passport drew her sharply back to reality. She had been beginning to feel too comfortable – and that was dangerous. "Well, if you've finished your coffee, I'll wash up," she announced briskly, rising to her feet. "It's time I was getting back downstairs. I have work to do."

"That's a pity."

She was far too aware of his eyes watching her as she collected his mug and took it with her own to the pantry, far too aware that he had followed her and was standing in the doorway, leaning casually against the jamb, effectively blocking her in there.

She did her best to ignore him as she deftly dismantled the coffee-maker and dropped everything into the sink, and turned on the hot water tap. But eventually the tension became too much.

"Do you enjoy watching me skivvying for you?" she challenged.

"There is an alternative," he suggested, his voice as soft as velvet.

"What's that?" she queried tartly. "The brig?"

He laughed. "I have a large and extremely comfortable bed. You'd be more than welcome to share it."

"You mean earn my passage on my back, instead of skivvying?" she retorted. "Thanks, but no thanks. I'd prefer the brig."

"I don't think you mean that." He had moved in close behind her, placing his hands against the sink on each side of her waist – trapping her, though she knew she could easily escape. She felt a shimmer of heat run through her as his head bent slowly towards her, felt his breath hot on the nape of her neck. "I really don't think you mean that," he murmured.

Temptation was like an ache inside her. Fevered images filled her mind, of his hands on her naked body, his scorching kisses igniting every inch of her skin…

He turned her in his arms and his mouth claimed hers, both tender and demanding, his hot tongue seeking all the sweet, secret corners of her mouth. Her senses were reeling, and she could only respond, the heat inside her pooling like molten gold in the pit of her stomach.

She became aware that he had unfastened some of the buttons down the front of her white shirt, and slid his hand inside to curve over the ripe swell of her breast. A small moan of pleasure escaped her lips as his mouth broke from hers, and began to trace hot kisses down the slender column of her throat.

The musky scent of his skin was drugging her mind, and some deep, feminine core inside her, beyond the reach of reason, was urging her to surrender…

But some last shred of sanity pulled her back from the brink. With a sharp twist she broke free of him.

"Actually I do mean it," she asserted, her fingers fumbling as she struggled to fasten the buttons on her shirt. "I've no intention of being your plaything – I'll work my passage as a skivvy, thank you very much."

He mouth curved into a sardonic smile. "That might be a little more convincing if your body was conveying the same message," he taunted.

"You might be a little easier to convince if you weren't such an arrogant jerk!"

He laughed aloud at that. "You really put me in my place, don't you?" He moved away to sit on the arm of one of the sofas. "You may not believe me, but what just happened… That wasn't the reason I wanted to talk to you this evening."

"Oh?"

"Do you dive?"

"What?" She turned to him, startled by the sudden change of subject.

"Scuba diving."

"Well… yes, I do," she conceded.

"You're Open Water certified?"

"I'm PADI Divemaster certified," she asserted, tilting up her chin.

"Do you fancy coming down tomorrow?" he asked. "There's a sunken temple just off an island not far from here. I've been planning to explore it for a while."

Kat hesitated. She couldn't deny that she was tempted. She loved diving, and had thought several times on this trip that it would be good to get down and see what was beneath the sapphire surface of the sea. And a sunken temple…

"It should be interesting," he coaxed. "It dates from at least 1600 BC."

"Well, I…" Of course she shouldn't go. "I'll have to check the crew rota."

"Don't worry, I'll clear it with Maggie. Shall we say twelve o'clock?"

She *really* shouldn't go. "…OK."

He nodded. "I'll see you at twelve, down at the tender-dock."

## CHAPTER SEVEN

TO JUDGE from the groans and pale faces around the breakfast table in the crew mess, it had been a good night ashore. Kat had been careful not to wake Gill when she had slid out of her bunk – she had been snoring quietly, her make-up smeared all over her face and still wearing the pink dress she had gone out in.

But the First Mate was showing no mercy. "Come on, people, get moving," he ordered, clapping his hands loudly.

More groans – though discreet.

"There are covers to fit, brasses to polish. Dougie, if you want to get your Deck Officer Certificate, you'd better come up and join me on the bridge while I plot our course. In case none of you have noticed, it's a new day, we have guests aboard, and we're heading south."

"The man's a sadist," Dougie muttered as he levered himself heavily to his feet.

But the crew were far too professional to linger. Even Gill managed to stumble to the table, where the Sous-Chef very gently placed a tumbler in front of her. "Drink it," he urged. "It's my own recipe. Cures anything."

"If it doesn't kill you," one of the others put in.

Whatever was in it, it seemed to do the trick. A short time later Gill was able to manage a weak nod of agreement as Maggie read off the day's work roster.

"I'll give you a hand with the guest staterooms," Kat offered quietly.

"But you're not on until the late shift."

"That's OK. You can pay me back the favour another time."

Gill leaned sideways and dropped her head on Kat's shoulder. "Thanks – you're a real pal."

"At least there's only three of them to do – it shouldn't take too long."

"That," declared Gill with weary foreboding, "is the triumph of hope over experience!"

The accommodation deck was quiet as the two girls wheeled the housekeeping trolley along the passage – Maggie was always insistent that they wait until they were sure the guests were out of their staterooms before going in to clean them.

"Might as well do Princess Twinkle-Toes first – get it over with," Gill suggested, tapping on the door. There was no reply, so she opened it using the over-ride fob which unlocked every door on the deck. "Oh God…"

The suite was a mess. There was make-up on the bedding, dark hair-extensions on the floor, and dirty tissues in the sink. The cloying smell of a dozen hair and beauty products pervaded the air.

"Yuk!" Kat wrinkled her nose. "It gets worse every day."

Gill stood for a moment on the threshold, a steadying hand on the door-jamb. "I think… I'm going to be sick," she muttered, her face so pale it was almost green.

Kat turned to her in concern. "Look, you pop downstairs and take some Milk-of-Magnesia or something. Have a lie down for a bit if you need to. I'll make a start in here."

"Are you sure?" Gill's eyes conveyed her gratitude. "I won't be long, I promise."

Left alone, Kat cast a jaded eye around the room. It was so bad, it almost looked as if it had been done deliberately – but more likely Stasia was simply spoiled, used to having someone to pick up after her all the time.

With a small shrug of her shoulders she began to unsnap the cover of the grubby duvet and pull it off.

She was in the bathroom scrubbing at the stained sink when she heard a commotion from the bedroom. "*Viakas*!" The raw Greek expletive was followed by the sound of someone kicking the housekeeping trolley. "Who left this here?"

Kat saw her reflection in the bathroom mirror roll her eyes and pin on a brittle smile. "I'm sorry…" she said, stepping into the bedroom.

"Get it out of here," Stasia spat. "It's in the way. And so are you - servants aren't allowed in the staterooms when guests are around."

Kat drew in a steadying breath. "I'm sorry, I thought…"

"You're not paid to think," Stasia snarled. "Just get out - and take this with you." She kicked the trolley again.

*Don't say anything, don't react*, Kat warned herself. Focussing on holding herself very erect, not even looking at the other girl, she walked from the room, drawing the trolley with her.

"Wait."

Kat paused in the doorway.

"Pick that up."

Stasia was pointing imperiously at a tin of furniture polish which must have fallen from the trolley when she had kicked it. Kat clenched and unclenched her fist, forcing herself to breathe slowly as she walked back into the room and snatched up the tin from the floor.

As she turned, she found Stasia standing in the doorway, evidently intent on preventing her from obeying her earlier order to leave. The girl looked her up and down slowly, her lip curling in arrogant disdain.

"You're the one with a crush on Javier, aren't you?" she sneered. "I've seen it in your eyes, the way you look at him. Well, you're wasting your time." She tossed her long black hair back over her shoulder. "He's never going to be interested in the likes of you."

Kat could feel the heat of anger rising inside her. *Don't react*, she told herself firmly. *If you lose your temper, she wins.*

"I just thought I'd give you the warning – girl to girl." That smile was as venomous as a Coral Snake. "Oh, and if you're wondering what he's like in bed," she added, stepping aside from the door, "he's *amazing.*"

Kat stood in the tiny en-suite bathroom of her crew-cabin, regarding her own reflection in the mirror. Stasia's words had hit home: '*You've got a crush on him... He's never going to be interested in the likes of you...*'

Of course he wouldn't - she had already known that. It was all just a game to him, seducing one of his crew. And as Gill had warned her, crew-girls who let themselves be seduced by yacht-owners were asking for trouble.

But Stasia... That hint about having slept with Javier – was that the truth? Javier had certainly implied that he wasn't interested in sleeping with her, but he hadn't outright denied it. She wouldn't put it past him – Stasia was only a year younger than Amy.

*Amy,* she reminded herself. That was why she was here. She really didn't care whether he had slept with Stasia or not.

The question she had to decide right now was whether she was going to go diving with him this afternoon. Maybe it wasn't the wisest thing to do - she hadn't even checked if anyone else was going.

But dammit, why shouldn't she go? She wasn't afraid of him - she knew she could take care of herself if necessary. And if she never took the risk of getting closer to him, she would never have a chance to get the evidence she needed.

Besides, she really was tempted by the thought of diving down to a sunken temple. The idea had always intrigued her. She had dived a few wrecks and found them fascinating, but a temple was something else.

Why should she let Stasia put her off?

Her swimsuit was dry from yesterday, and she wriggled into it, pulling on a pair of navy-blue shorts and a turquoise T-shirt over the top – purchased, like the swimsuit, from the yacht's well-stocked stores.

Bundling up her hair into its usual top-knot with a blue scrunchy, she slipped her feet into a pair of flip-flops and took one last look at herself in the small mirror propped above the sink.

"Look, the only reason he's coming on to you is because he comes on to every female he sees," she warned herself firmly. "Don't start thinking there's anything special about it, because there ain't. Like he's really going to be interested in you? As long as you give him the message loud and clear that you're not up for being a playboy's play-toy, he'll give up and move on. And that's exactly what you want - right? So..." She drew in a long, deep breath, squaring her shoulders. "Let's go diving."

The tender dock was on one of the lower decks, but the side hatch was open, allowing bright sunshine to spill in. Javier was already there, and greeted her with a faintly mocking smile, as if he had known just how unsure she had been about whether she would come.

"Good morning. It's a lovely day for a dive – the visibility should be excellent."

"I'm looking forward to it," she responded coolly.

"Good. Chose a wet-suit." He indicated one of the open equipment cupboards at the side of the dock. "There's a good selection – you should find one that will fit you."

"Thank you."

She glanced through the rail of wet-suits hanging like shrugged-off skins, picking out a couple to compare for the best size. Joe, the second mate, and a couple of the deckhands were loading the diving equipment into the tender, then swung it out on its davits and lowered it to smoothly to the sea.

A short ladder was thrown down to the deck, and Javier stepped down, offering Kat his hand to help her. She took it for the minimal possible time, steadying herself quickly – the tender, being so much smaller, was being rocked about by the waves which didn't even register on the yacht, the effect multiplied by the backwash from the white hull rising steeply above them.

"Who else is coming?" she asked, keeping her voice as casual as possible.

"No-one." Those dark eyes challenged her. "Is that a problem?"

She shrugged her slim shoulders, feigning unconcern. "Of course not. Why would it be?"

A quirk of a smile curved that intriguing mouth. "No reason."

Joe and one of the deckhands had followed them down onto the tender. With the cables from the davits released, Joe gunned the engine, and they nosed out into open water.

The yacht had moved from Mykonos during the night. They were now moored in a tranquil bay enclosed by the arms of a small rocky island, its slopes draped in blue-green cypress and tall green pines. There appeared to be no houses, but she could see the weathered stone pillars of an ancient temple on the shoulder of the hill.

"That's the temple which was probably built after the original was submerged," Javier told her.

"What caused it to submerge?"

"Possibly the eruption of Santorini. A lot of the coastal waters around here have evidence of sunken villages - paving, temples - dated to around that period. It's fascinating."

The tender was gathering speed, the wind whipping Kat's hair and rapidly unravelling her top-knot. She pushed the curling strands impatiently from her eyes, keeping her gaze fixed on the temple and doing her best to ignore the fact that Javier was standing quite close behind her.

They swept in a smooth curve around the headland and into the next bay. The slopes here were lower, and a ribbon of smooth pale sand marked the water's edge. The water was a lot shallower – she could see the rocks and sand of the bottom, and schools of bright fish dodging among the drifting sea-weed.

She had been a little suspicious about why the yacht had moored in the other bay, but now she could see that the draft here would be nowhere near deep enough for her.

Joe cut the engine and the deckhand dropped the anchor. With the boat rocking gently on the swell, Kat turned her back on Javier and quickly stripped off her T-shirt and shorts, and sat down to pull on her wet-suit, easing it up over her body and sliding her arms into the sleeves.

"We only need to go down to about ten metres," Javier explained, "so we'll be using compressed air, not EAN."

She nodded, zipping up her suit and trying not to notice how well he fitted his. Custom made, of course, moulding those wide shoulders and lean torso, and hugging closely around… Yes, well, it was a good fit, she acknowledged a little breathlessly, bending her head quickly over her air-tanks to test the regulator.

He may be something of a playboy, but she noticed with satisfaction that a casual attitude didn't extend to his diving. He was meticulously efficient in checking both her equipment and his own, before Joe lifted their tanks onto their backs and handed them their weight belts, diving knives and snorkels.

As she strapped her dive computer to her wrist, he handed her a small black gizmo. "Ever used one of these?"

"What is it?"

"It's a transceiver – it enables us to talk to each other while we're down."

"Wow!" She turned it over in her hand. It was very small, smaller than a packet of cigarettes. "I've heard of them, but I've never seen one."

"You fix it to the strap of your mask, so it lies against the side of your head." He showed her how. "It picks up what you are saying through the vibrations in your bone. It's got digital speech processing, but it can still be a bit garbled with your regulator in. It's easy enough to use – you tap it here to transmit, and tap it again to receive. It can pick up a signal pretty well up to a couple of hundred metres in these conditions, and it's in continual contact with the set here on the boat."

She rolled her eyes expressively. "Ah – the wonders of modern technology!"

He checked the dive computer on his wrist. "I have twenty five minutes past twelve," he said.

"OK." She synchronised her time with his, then leaned over the side to sluice her face-mask and flippers in the water before putting them on.

"Ready?" he asked.

"Ready," she confirmed briskly.

She stepped over the transom onto the swim platform, fitted her snorkel into her mouth, and tipped forward to roll smoothly into the water, somersaulting well clear of the boat.

She was tumbling in a world of luminous green and shining bubbles, a cacophony of roarings and metallic clankings in her ears.

She uncurled herself slowly, amused as always by the wobbling, saucer-shaped bubbles rising in front of her. She used them to orientate herself to the surface, drifting slowly upwards, playfully popping bubbles with her finger as she went and watching as each one shattered into a dozen tiny replicas of itself.

She broke the water, blinking in the strong sunlight, and pushed back the wayward strands of hair from her face. Treading water, she cleared her snorkel and face-mask, and gave the thumbs-up sign to Joe as he waved to her from the boat. Javier had surfaced beside her.

"OK?"

"OK."

"Follow me. We can snorkel over to the site. It's not far, but it'll save dive time."

The mid-day sunlight was streaming almost directly down into the clear water, casting ever-shifting patterns of light across the sandy bottom. Shoals of brightly-coloured fish darted between clumps of sea-weed, while among the rocks sea anemones waved their purple-tipped tentacles.

They had swum for a few minutes when she noticed several strange dark shapes looming through the water ahead of them. Javier paused, and she swam up beside him, removing her snorkel. "This is it?" she asked, feeling a surge of excitement.

"This is it."

They both fitted their regulators and turned on their air supply. "Try your transceiver."

Kat blinked, startled by the sound of his voice in her ear. It sounded slightly odd, as if muffled by a blanket, but distinct enough to hear.

"Can you hear me? Tap it to switch to transmit."

She tapped it as he had shown her. "Yes I…" It was awkward to speak with the regulator in her mouth – she sounded like an amateur ventriloquist, struggling with m's and b's. Then she realised that she didn't need to speak aloud, just form the words silently, as if she was whispering. "Yes, I can hear you fine! This is one very clever piece of kit."

"Very useful, too," he concurred. "Come on, let's go down."

She let a little air out of her buoyancy jacket, then tipped over head first and finned slowly down to the ruins.

An incredible sight met her eyes - huge blocks of carved stone, walls and pavements, statues and archways. She followed Javier, gazing in wonder at the scene which materialised around her.

It was almost surreal - shafts of sunlight slanted down through the green water, fish darted where once the acolytes of some long-forgotten god or goddess had acted out their solemn ceremonials.

"Wow – this is amazing!"
"Worth coming to see?"
"Oh yes."
"There's lots more - this way."

They swam on, as on each side of them rose avenues of slender columns extending into the distance. Kat felt like some kind of strange bird, soaring and swooping freely in three-dimensional space, no longer bound by gravity.

Some of the columns were still standing almost complete, many were tumbled or broken in half by the earthquake or whatever it was that had caused the temple to sink beneath the waves.

The tops of some of the fallen columns were intricately carved with leaves. She swam closer, touching down on the sandy bottom to study them, brushing aside a strand of seaweed. "Come and look at this," she enthused. "The detail is absolutely incredible, even after all this time."

He came over to join her, swimming down beside her – she was so absorbed in what she was looking at that she had forgotten to be wary of him.

"They're really well preserved. You'd think they'd be more eroded."

"It's quite a sheltered bay," he explained. "It keeps out the worst of the storms, plus there's not much tide."

She pulled aside a little more sea-weed to get a better look, but suddenly Javier caught her arm. "Careful..."

He pointed to a dark shadow beneath the column. She recognised it instantly – the distinctive narrow head of a Moray Eel. She drew back – though Morays were not usually as dangerous as their reputation suggested, it was always best to be circumspect.

Leaving the eel to his silent watch for prey, they swam on. A cloud of tiny neon-blue damselfish didn't seem bothered by her presence at all. Schools of striped sea bream sailed past, a couple of crabs scuttled around on the bottom, a bright orange blenny regarded her with a suspicious eye from his hiding place among the corals.

She had loved diving since she had first tried it, on a school trip to Cornwall when she was fifteen – the sense of freedom, of being able to move in three dimensions as if she was flying.

And it was so peaceful – though not silent. She could hear the sound of her own rhythmic breathing and the regular gurgling of bubbles as she breathed out, she could hear the swish of water swirling around the ruins, the clicking and popping and crunching of all the marine creatures going about their daily business down here in their own world.

She was enjoying herself so much, she had forgotten any reservations she had had about Javier. Down here, he was her dive buddy, not her enemy.

He was investigating something, and she swam over to look. A massive statue was lying on its back, half covered in a tangle of seaweed. She helped him brush aside the debris to reveal a face, strong and serene, beautiful.

"I wonder how many people have seen this?" she mused.

"It's quite unlikely that anyone's seen it for more than three and a half thousand years."

She turned to him, her eyes bright with excitement behind her mask. "Really? The site is secret?"

He shook his head. "It's not secret, but it isn't listed."

"How did you find out about it?"

"I'll tell you when we get topside." He glanced at his dive computer. "It's about time we were going up."

"Right."

She was reluctant to leave, but knew the necessity of keeping to the safety rules. Adjusting her buoyancy jacket again, she let herself drift slowly up to a few metres below the surface.

Hanging there to wait out the decompression time, she watched in idle fascination as a copper-brown stingray undulated lazily across the sea-bottom, looking for lunch. She was glad she had set aside her reservations – it had been worth coming.

Javier floated lazily, balanced by his buoyancy jacket, watching Kat as she drifted a few feet away from him. She was so graceful, so at home in the water, as if it was her natural element.

But he had been impressed, too, by her practiced efficiency, her disciplined attention to every safety detail. Not surprised, just impressed.

He had to admit, she was getting to him. It wasn't just that slender body, with its subtle but temptingly feminine curves, nor that bright mop of copper curls. Nor even those beautiful silk-fringed grey-green eyes.

It was in the way she laughed, the way she could charm even his hard-bitten security chief, the way she challenged him at every turn instead of trying to turn him up sweet.

He'd never known a woman quite like her. She'd probably tell him he'd been moving in the wrong circles, he reflected with a short laugh...

"What...?" She had turned suddenly, and he realised that he had had his transceiver set to transmit. "Sorry, I didn't catch what you said."

"Nothing." It was fortunate that he hadn't been thinking aloud, he reflected wryly. "Time to go ashore."

"Good. I'm starving!"

Kat slipped off her flippers as soon as the water was shallow enough to wade - there was just no way you could walk elegantly in flippers. The tender had pulled in close to the shore, and the deckhand was in the water, conveying a picnic basket to the beach.

Javier paused by the boat's swim-platform, shrugging off his air tanks and leaving them there with his other equipment, so she did the same, unzipping her wet-suit and peeling it off. The deckhand swung himself back aboard, and to her surprise Joe gunned the engine and the boat took off back towards the headland.

"What... Where are they going?" she demanded suspiciously.

"They're taking the wet-suits back to get them washed," he explained casually. "They'll be back to pick us up after lunch."

"Oh..." She wasn't sure she would have agreed to have lunch alone with him if he had asked her in advance – which was probably why he hadn't, she surmised grimly. But it would probably be better to act cool, rather than kick up a fuss. "Fine."

She was struggling not to take too much notice of the fact that he was wearing only a pair of black lycra swimming shorts. She had already seen the back view, though now she had the chance to appreciate more fully the smooth muscle beneath his wide shoulders, the lean taper of his torso down to... phew... that tight, hard butt she had glimpsed so briefly.

But when he turned... That hard chest, covered with just a smattering of dark, rough, curling hair, the sculpted ridges of his abdomen, the...

Her breath hitched in her throat, and she had to pretend a sudden need to remove a stone from between her toes.

"There should be a comb in the basket, and some sun-cream if you want it," he said as he followed her up the beach.

"Thank you." She hurried ahead, pulling the scrunchy from her hair and letting it fall loose around her shoulders, curling wildly.

"If you want some help rubbing it in..."

Of course - she should have guessed there would be an ulterior motive. "I can probably manage well enough, thank you," she responded with cool dignity.

He returned her a smile that was laced with sardonic humour – she chose to ignore it.

The sun cream was Factor 30, a very expensive brand. She squirted a large dollop into her palm and smoothed it onto her legs, conscious of him watching her.

So let him watch, she accorded dismissively. When she was fifteen she had been embarrassed about her body – too conscious of her height, and how skinny she was. But she had got over that a long time ago. Now... well, she quite liked it.

And so, it seemed, did he.

Javier leaned back against the warm rock, watching in amusement as Kat dived into the picnic basket for another taco wrap. She bit into it with hard white teeth, and a healthy disregard for calories.

"So..." She paused between bites. "You were going to tell me how you knew about the temple."

He was tempted to lean forward and lick a wayward trickle of jalapeño sauce from her chin, but he wasn't going to risk the careful progress he was making by rushing his fences. "I'm a patron of a conservation group that's trying to save the monk seals," he explained, reaching for a taco himself. "They're one of the most endangered species in the world."

She nodded. "I heard that."

"They used to rear their young on the beaches, but they're quite shy, they don't like to be disturbed. Unfortunately the growth of tourism has meant that they've lost their habitat, so they've moved into using sea-caves. The problem is that when there's a storm the young cubs get washed away. More than half don't make it to two months old."

"Oh, the poor little things!" She lowered her taco, those amazing grey-green eyes wide and sparkling with instant tears.

Javier felt suddenly a little light-headed, as if she was reaching right into his chest and squeezing his heart. No - it was probably just indigestion, he told himself firmly. Those tacos were pretty spicy.

"We've set up a project to look for places that can be protected, where they can be encouraged to set up new colonies."

"And this island is one of them?" Her interest appeared quite genuine. He liked that - by this point, a lot of people were beginning to glaze over.

"It's a definite possibility," he concurred. "And finding the temple is a bonus – we may also be able to get it protected as a National Heritage site."

"Killing two birds with one stone!" she concluded with gurgle of laughter.

It wasn't indigestion. She really was gorgeous when she laughed – he wanted to see her laugh like that all the time…

Forcing himself to stop looking at her, he reached for a can of soda, popped the tab and tipped his head back to let it pour down his throat. He had promised himself that he would take it slowly – she was still ready to break his arm if he made a wrong move. But it was going to take a great deal of self-control.

Especially when she was sitting there in that blue swimsuit that clung to her like a second skin, moulding every tempting curve of that slender body…

Kate lay back on the sand and closed her eyes with a sigh. After the past couple of weeks spent at the beck and call of Javier's demanding guests, that dive had ironed all the kinks out of her body, leaving her with a feeling of utter relaxation.

The only sounds were the lapping of the waves shushing gently over the tiny pebbles of the beach, a bumble-bee searching for nectar around a gorse bush somewhere nearby, and the more distant twittering of the birds.

This had to be closest thing to heaven – sun, sea… And Javier close beside her.

But that was a temptation she had to resist, she reminded herself with a trace of regret. Even if the memory of the way he had kissed her lingered on her lips, staying with her as she drifted on the fringes of sleep…

She jerked sharply awake as the loud roar of a motorbike split the air. Impossible…

A bright red jet-ski was swooping in across the bay. It swerved into the shallows, sending up a tsunami of spray. Almost before it had stopped Stasia, in that fluorescent yellow bikini, jumped off and stomped up beach, pointing angrily at Kat and letting forth a rapid torrent of Greek – it wasn't necessary to understand the language to make a good guess at what she was saying.

"We've been diving," Javier responded in English, unruffled in the face of the girl's incendiary rage.

"With *her*?"

The contempt in her voice would have stripped paint. Kat had to dig her fingernails painfully into the palm of her hand to stop herself responding in kind.

"She's a very experienced diver."

"What about Jasen?" Stasia challenged, her eyes flashing. "You could have invited him."

"Thank you." Javier smiled thinly. "I'd prefer to live a little longer."

"He's a perfectly competent diver," she insisted.

"He dives like he drives – recklessly."

Stasia launched into another stream of virulent Greek, her hands clenched into fists, angry tears spilling down her cheeks. It was clear that she felt some kind of entitlement - was Javier gaming both of them?

After a moment he sighed with weary patience and rose to his feet, putting his arms around the young girl. She rested her head against his chest – but Kat couldn't miss the glitter of triumph in the glance Stasia shafted in her direction.

*So this was supposed to be a competition? Who fired the starting gun?*

Javier offered her a smile which she guessed was supposed to convey regret. "I'm sorry – I have to take Stasia back to the boat," he said. "The tender will be back in a few minutes to pick you up. We'll… talk later."

"Fine." She shrugged her slender shoulders in a gesture of unconcern. "There's no rush – I'm enjoying the sun." She lay back in the sand, folding her hands behind her head, closing her eyes – apart from a tiny crack through which she watched him help Stasia onto the jet-ski, where she settled behind him, hugging her arms around his waist and resting her cheek against his bare back.

So what was that all about? Kat mused as she watched the jet-ski swing out across the bay. In spite of everything, she couldn't help but feel a little sorry for the girl. Like Amy, she was far too young and naïve to handle a ruthless operator like Javier de Almanzor.

Although… it really wouldn't surprise her if he intended to marry Stasia – though maybe not yet. It would be exactly the sort of dynastic marriage men like him entered into, combining two substantial financial empires.

Meanwhile, he would be stringing her along, while he enjoyed as many casual flings as he liked. Unfortunately for him, he had got caught out on this occasion.

Which cast her in the role of the casual fling. Well, of course she was. Men like him didn't take women like her seriously. They were purely for amusement. When it came to the crunch, he would inevitably choose the woman who best suited his long-term interests.

Leaving his casual fling behind with the debris of their picnic lunch, to be collected when convenient.

## CHAPTER EIGHT

JAVIER had hoped for a chance to speak to Kat when she got back to the yacht, but he was detained by an urgent call from New York, and by the time he got down to the tender garage the deckhands were finishing stowing the equipment, and there was no sign of her.

He didn't see her again until dinner, and then there was no opportunity for a private moment as she was serving at the table. He tried to catch her eye but she resolutely refused to let him. He really wasn't surprised that she was upset, but he had done his best to deal with an unpleasant situation, removing Stasia before she blew a fuse.

He watched as she moved around the table, poised and graceful, immaculate in her smart, slightly masculine uniform. But he could still see as if etched on his retina the image of how she had looked down on the beach - those long slender legs stretched out in front of her, that smoothly curving backside as she dipped to remove her swim-fins.

Those perfect breasts, quite small, but firm and ripe, tipped with hard little nubs that had been so clearly visible through the taut, damp fabric of her swim-suit...

"...didn't you, Javier?"

He glanced around, startled. He hadn't heard a word Stasia had been saying. "I did?" he responded blandly. "If you say so, I'm sure I must have done."

Her petulant little mouth hardened into a thin line. "You weren't even listening," she protested.

"I'm sorry." He offered her a placating smile. "I was momentarily distracted."

She glared at him, but said no more, returning her attention to toying rather sulkily with the food on her plate. But the respite was short-lived. The storm was foreshadowed by the glittering hostility in her eyes as they followed Kat, who had just finished drizzling vinaigrette onto Talia's feta salad.

Suddenly she tapped her water-glass with a knife. "You, girl," she demanded in an imperious tone. "Refill my glass."

Kat didn't flinch, though her eyes sparked with a dangerous anger. Maybe only Javier understood that it was the self-control instilled by her martial arts training which enabled her to maintain that cool restraint. Her face was carefully ironed of all expression as she stepped forward with a water jug and filled Stasia's glass to the prescribed three-quarters full, careful not to spill a drop.

Stasia turned back, and her face distorted. "You stupid bitch!" she spat. "I wanted more wine, not water." And snatching up her glass she tossed the contents straight into Kat's face.

A moment of startled silence - then shock erupted around the table. Maggie, the chief stewardess, stepped in swiftly to hustle Kat away. Some of the water had splashed Talia, who was protesting loudly, dabbing at the front of her dress with a napkin.

Fedor rose quickly to his feet. "Stasia! How dare you? You were not brought up to behave in that way. Go to your room at once."

Stasia slammed one clenched fist on the table. "No! Don't you speak to me like that, Papa. I'm not going to be sent to my room like a child."

"You're behaving like one," Fedor returned coldly. "Apologise to your step-mother at once, and then leave the table. I do not wish to see you again until you are ready to behave like a civilised woman, not a little harridan."

Tears sprang to the young girl's eyes, and she shoved her chair aside, storming from the dining-saloon.

The tension around the table slowly subsided. Fedor puffed out a breath and sat down. "I am sorry, my friend." He shook his head at Javier. "She is… a little highly strung."

Javier smiled wryly. He felt almost sorry for the girl. Fedor was a doting father, but he was inclined to swing between wildly spoiling both his children and laying down the law with a heavy hand, never letting them forget who held the purse strings.

He was well aware that one of the main reasons his friend had brought his family along on what was essentially a business trip was in the hope of promoting a dynastic alliance, but it was never going to happen. He had always tried to be careful not to encourage the idea, and particularly not to give Stasia the wrong impression.

But Stasia was young, and could be volatile. He could only hope that she wouldn't do anything stupid.

Kat let Gill hustle her downstairs to the crew quarters on the lower deck. She was more shocked than angry now. Wiping the water from her face, she laughed in disbelief. "Well – I don't know what that was all about!"

"You don't?" Gill challenged her, her eyes serious. "She's jealous, is what. You went diving with Javier this afternoon. Oh Kat, I warned you never to get involved with a boat-owner."

"I'm not involved with him," Kat protested, though she suspected the hint of pink in her cheeks might betray her. "He wanted to go diving, that's all. There's a... a place he wanted to explore. And you know you never dive alone, for safety reasons, so..."

"And the fact that there are at least eight other members of the crew who could have gone with him – people he frequently dives with?"

"Well, I don't know why he invited me," Kat insisted evasively. "He just did. And I really enjoy diving, so I said yes."

Gill shook her head. "Oh, sweetheart – you can try to fool yourself, but you can't fool me. He's got the hots for you – you can see it every time he looks at you. And you can play the butter-wouldn't-melt act all you like, but you feel the same about him. Well, who wouldn't? But you know you'll only get hurt."

"Oh, I know," Kat conceded with a sigh. "None better. But honestly, Gill, I may find him attractive but I'm not going to let it go any further."

Gill laughed dryly. "Well, good luck with that. And if I were you, I'd steer well clear of Stasia, too. Fortunately they're leaving tomorrow, so we won't have to put up with her for much longer."

Kat rolled her eyes in heartfelt relief. "Thank heavens for small mercies!"

♥

Maggie was of the same mind as Gill. Allocating the day's tasks at breakfast the next morning, she slanted Kat a quizzical look. "Kat, you'd better switch to the laundry today. I know what happened last night wasn't your fault, but it's probably best if you stay out of the way for a while."

Kat nodded agreement. "That's fine by me," she conceded wryly. The laundry was one of the least popular jobs, down on the service deck with no view of the sky. With two industrial scale washing machines and three large dryers, as well as a big rotary iron for sheets, the laundry-room was cramped and hot.

But a morning buried under a mountain of towels, sheets and crew t-shirts was a good enough way to stay out of Stasia's way – and to stay out of Javier's way too.

It was tiring work, loading and unloading washing machines, ironing sheets and sorting underpants – hot and thirsty too. After a couple of hours, Kat felt she deserved a break and some fresh air.

Slipping up the aft stairs to the crew quarters, she got herself a tall glass of ice-cold orange juice from the fridge, then climbed to the accommodation deck and stepped out into the sunshine.

She leaned against the railing and breathed in luxuriantly. The yacht looked beautiful, all smooth white curves and gleaming glass as it cleaved through the glittering jewel-bright sea.

For all the stresses and drama, she had enjoyed the past few weeks. There was a pleasant camaraderie among the crew, she had seen some fabulous sights, and had had the chance to try out some of the yacht's collection of 'toys.'

And it had given her the chance to be close to Javier.

Drawing in a long, deep breath, she closed her eyes. Gill's words had been spinning in her brain since last night. She knew that Javier had the 'hots' for her – that somewhat inelegant term just about described it. He wanted to get her into bed – and the fact that she hadn't instantly fallen for his practiced seduction had piqued his interest in the chase.

But she was a little surprised that he had let it be obvious enough that Gill had been able to spot it.

And for herself... Dammit, she couldn't deny the temptation. He was one hunk of gorgeous male – to the memory of him standing naked in the shower was now added the memory of him on that secluded beach, all hard muscle and sun-bronzed skin...

But that wasn't all. He was quick and intelligent, with the sort of dry sense of humour she enjoyed. And he was clearly a good employer – every single member of the crew spoke highly of him. And the fact that people trusted him - hard-headed businessmen - over deals worth millions of dollars...

*Stop it* she warned herself fiercely. He might be all of those things, but he was still the sleaze-bag who had seduced and dumped Amy.

But try as she might to push it from her mind, the memory of the way he had kissed her still lingered...

"There you are. I've been looking for you." She turned sharply, startled – it was as if her own wayward fantasies had conjured him right there in front of her. "We need to talk."

"I don't think so." She stepped back, trying to evade him, but found herself cornered against the bulkhead.

"We do," he insisted softly. "What happened yesterday…"

"There's no need to explain that." Wounded pride lent a defiant tilt to her chin. "Although… yes, there is." She found the courage to confront him directly. "Why did you invite me to go with you, when you could have taken any one of a dozen members of the crew?"

He acknowledged the question with a wry smile. "I wanted to spend some time with you. I thought… I hoped… maybe we could be… friends."

"Friends?" Her voice echoed her disbelief.

"Alright - more than friends." That velvet voice, those dark, dark eyes were weaving spells around her.

"Wh… What about Stasia?" she demanded raggedly.

He shook his head in firm denial. "Stasia is the daughter of a close business associate – nothing more."

"Oh?" Her eyes flashed ice. "Funny – she told me you were pretty good in bed. Her exact word was 'amazing.'"

He frowned, then laughed, shaking his head. "She's making it up. I have never slept with Stasia. I'm just not interested."

There was a deep note of sincerity in his voice which almost had her believing him.

"I should have guessed she would follow us yesterday if she found out where we had gone. I'm afraid she's had something of a crush on me since she was fifteen years old."

"Something of a crush?" Kat repeated, laughing at his understatement. "She has all the makings of a bunny-boiler!"

"She's used to getting her own way," Javier concurred. "Her father spoils her, and she winds him around her little finger. Unfortunately I suspect he may have encouraged her to think in terms of a marriage between us, but that was never going to happen."

"And yet you left me behind on the beach to be collected like a piece of discarded luggage, and brought her back to the boat." She hoped she didn't sound as pathetically hurt as she felt.

"I'm sorry. I needed to calm her down – she was working herself up into a major tantrum. I've seen her make herself sick when she gets like that. I wanted to speak to you as soon as you got back, but I couldn't find you. And then it was dinner time..." He sighed. "I'm afraid her jealousy got the better of her."

"There's no reason for her to be jealous," she protested weakly.

"Oh, there probably is..." He had moved closer again, trapping her against the bulkhead. "Will I be taking my life in my hands if I kiss you?" he murmured on a note of teasing humour. "You won't throw me overboard?"

Kat felt something constricting her throat. When he gazed down into her eyes like this, she felt as if the whole world was slipping away. "I'm... not making any promises," she responded, struggling to match his light tone.

"Good." He laughed softly. "I've always enjoyed living dangerously."

He put his hand along her cheek, and bent his head slowly towards hers. Her lashes fluttered down over her eyes - she knew she should be resisting him, but her willpower seemed to have been blown to the four winds.

All she wanted was to feel the warmth of his mouth on hers, the hard strength of his arms around her.

Their breath mingled in a moment of sweet anticipation, then with a small sigh her lips parted, and she felt his hot, moist tongue swirl over the sweet, sensitive membranes within before plundering deeper, into all the deepest, secret corners.

She felt herself grow dizzy, her pulse racing as her head tipped back. He was curving her intimately close, so that her breasts were crushed against the hard wall of his chest as his hand slid down the long curve of her spine to stroke over the smooth swell of her backside.

A fever had ignited in her blood, and she knew there was only one cure…

A sharp cry and the sound of running footsteps startled them both. Kat glanced up to see Stasia race up the steps to the main deck and into the saloon, slamming the door behind her.

"She saw us," she breathed.

"Don't worry about it…"

He tried to draw her back into his arms again, but this time she found the strength to hold him away. "No – I have to go," she insisted. "I have work to do."

For a moment she thought he wasn't going to release her, but then with some reluctance he stepped aside. "This isn't finished," he warned softly.

"Yes it is."

She hurried back down the stairs to the laundry-room and closed the door firmly behind her, leaning back against it and closing her eyes.

This was getting impossible. When he was close to her, she struggled to remember her own name, let alone why she was supposed to be here. And she had let him kiss her three – no four - times now. And each time the temptation to let it go further had been harder to resist.

And her dreams each night had been more and more vivid, so that she woke breathless and with her duvet kicked into a heap at the foot of her bunk, listening anxiously to make sure she hadn't woken Gill.

Last night she had dreamed they were on the beach…

*He reached out and caught her hand, drawing her towards him until she was straddled across his lap. She was a little shy when she realised she wasn't wearing her swimsuit, but he laughed teasingly at her blushes, holding her hands out wide so that she couldn't cover herself as his hot, dark gaze roved down over every inch of her naked body.*

*"It would have been naïve to think this wasn't inevitable," he murmured, wrapping her arms behind her and tipping her*

*back onto the warm sand, trapping her there so that his hand could wander freely over her soft, naked skin, circling the ripe, creamy swell of her breasts, teasing the tender pink nipples, then smoothing down over the curve of her stomach to dip between her slender thighs...*

With a grunt of impatience she shook the image from her brain, opening her eyes and forcing herself back to reality - back to the hot, brightly-lit laundry-room. This couldn't go on - she had to get off the boat, as soon as possible.

If only she could find a way to get her passport back...

By the middle of the afternoon Kat had a satisfying pile of freshly-ironed sheets and duvet covers to show for her hard work. Lifting them in her arms, she carried them out into the corridor and up the aft stairs to the linen cupboard on the accommodation deck.

Maggie was always very particular about keeping the linen cupboard tidy, so she was careful to lay them on the correct piles – sheets to the left, duvet covers to the...

A sudden commotion outside startled her. Loud voices - Stasia at full volume, others trying to calm her down. And then to her surprise she heard her own name.

Creeping to the door, she eased it open an inch. There were five or six people in the doorway to Stasia's stateroom. Maggie was there, and several other members of the crew, as well as Stasia's brother Jasen.

None of them were looking her way, so she took the opportunity to slip silently through the door and close it quietly behind her. She stepped away from it, schooling her face into an expression of innocent concern. As she moved into Stasia's eyeline, the girl shrieked and pointed at her accusingly.

"There she is. The thief! She stole them!"

Kat felt her cheeks go pale. "What? I haven't stolen anything."

"My earrings - my diamond earrings. She was in here cleaning yesterday – she must have stolen them then."

Kat shook her head. "I didn't." She drew in a steadying breath, standing up straight and squaring her shoulders. "I don't steal."

More people had arrived, craning to see what was happening. Bob, the head of security stepped forward, taking her arm in a firm grip. "You were cleaning the guest staterooms?" he demanded. "You're not supposed to be on this deck at all." His tone was accusatory.

"That wasn't on my orders."

Stasia had been looking rather pleased with herself, but at the sound of Javier's voice she began wailing hysterically again, throwing herself on his chest.

"It's her," she wept, milking the drama for all it was worth. "She's stolen my diamond earrings. My favourite diamond earrings – the ones Papa gave me for my birthday."

"I did not." Kat could feel her own hysteria rising. They were all looking at her, some with surprise, some with suspicion. "I'm not a thief. I've never stolen anything in my life."

Javier pulled Stasia's arms from around his neck and put her away from him, none too gently. "Stasia, I don't believe Kat has stolen anything from you," he stated firmly. "If you can't find your earrings, it will be simply because you have mislaid them. I suggest you look a little more thoroughly."

"I've looked! I've looked everywhere." Stasia sat down plump on the bed, her hands over her face, sobbing theatrically. "They've gone. She stole them. She's a thief – a dirty little thief."

"I'm not!" Acid tears were stinging the back of Kat's eyes, but she blinked them back fiercely – she was *not* going to cry! "I never even saw your stupid earrings."

Stasia was still shouting, everyone was talking at once, when a deep, sleepy voice cut into the commotion. "What is going on?" Emerging from her own stateroom on the opposite side of the passage, wrapped in a frothy green silk *peignoir*, Talia held up an imperious hand. "No, please do not all speak at once. Stasia, explain."

The girl lowered her hands – oddly, for all her histrionics, her eyes were quite clear and dry. "She stole my earrings," she insisted sulkily. "The ones Papa gave me for my birthday."

"Is this so?" Talia enquired of everyone in general.

"No, it isn't." It was Javier who replied, absolute certainty in his voice. "Stasia has made a mistake."

Talia sighed heavily. "For this I have been woken from my nap? Stasia, if you are wishing to cause trouble for somebody, you might at the least try a different trick. You have hidden the earrings yourself, just as you did before. Now go and fetch them, and let us have no more of this disturbance."

For a moment Stasia glared at her step-mother obstinately. Then with a flounce, she turned back into the room. She flung open her suitcase, pulled out a pair of shoes, and shook them out over the bed. Something sparkling fell onto the satin cover.

No-one said a word – they just stood staring at those bright points of light on the bed-cover. Stasia stormed into the suite's bathroom and slammed the door. Talia simply shrugged and turned away, her generous curves undulating as she strolled back into her own stateroom.

Kat felt the surge of hurt and rage roiling up inside her. She had thought she had learned long ago to control it, but now it was threatening to burst through. Her eyes were squeezed shut, her fists clenched; she wanted to scream, stamp her feet, hit something…

Instead she did the very thing she hadn't wanted to do. She burst into tears.

Javier was shocked by her reaction – his Kat wasn't the sort to cry. But this was no theatrical performance, like Stasia's – she was seriously distressed, great sobs tearing at her throat. There was more to it than simply the reaction to being falsely accused.

Scooping her up in his arms, he carried her into his stateroom.

Though she was so slender, she was no light weight, but he found he enjoyed the physical effort it took. As he set her down on the bed she curled up into a tight ball, her hair covering her face. He pulled a box of tissues from the nightstand and tucked a wad into her hand.

She mumbled something that sounded like, "Thank you."

He sat down on the bed beside her, gently stroking her hair. Normally he had an absolute horror of female tears – he suspected most men did. But this was different.

She snuffled a bit, then blew her nose loudly. That almost made him laugh. Only Kat would care so little about portraying an image of dainty femininity that she would make a noise like that!

"Thank you." She drew her hair aside and looked up at him with rain-soaked eyes. "You believed me."

"Of course I did." Yes, it really had been that simple. He hadn't had to think about it for a moment – he had instinctively known that she was telling the truth. She was no thief.

"I'm sorry." She sniffed, scrubbing at her face with the wad of tissues. "You must think I'm a real idiot, making a fuss like this."

"Not at all." He smiled down at her. "It was a pretty nasty thing to happen."

"It wasn't just what Stasia did." She hesitated. "It was… It brought back some bad memories."

He nodded to encourage her to continue. He had guessed there must be something like that in the background.

"There were some girls at school who were… horrible to me. I don't know why – they just ganged up on me. Well… I do know why. I'm dyslexic, and they'd picked on me since primary school, calling me stupid. And Ginge, because of my hair - and Olive Oyl because I'm so skinny."

He was going to protest at that, but it probably wasn't the right moment.

"Anyway, one time they played this trick on me." She drew in a deep breath before plunging on. "One of them hid her cell-phone in my school-bag, then made a big fuss about it being missing. One of the others called the number, and of course it rang in my bag."

She dabbed at her eyes again with the tissues.

"There was terrible trouble about it, the police were called in, everyone was calling me a thief." She shuddered. "It was only when my step-father insisted they dust it for fingerprints, and they found mine weren't on it, that anyone believed me."

"How old were you?"

"Twelve. I suppose I should have got over it by now, but..." The tears caught up with her again, coursing down her cheeks.

He gently prised the damp tissues from her hand, and replaced them with a fresh wad, then drew her onto his lap, rocking her gently as she rested her head against his shoulder.

"Those things aren't easy to get over."

There had been bullying at his own school, one of England's top public schools. He still vividly recalled one particular kid – Nigel. He was plump and had a stammer, and a small knot of particularly obnoxious boys had picked on him mercilessly.

He had watched it for a while, feeling increasingly angry. One afternoon after rugger practice they had begun flicking the poor lad with towels, laughing as they drove him into a cowering heap in the corner of the showers.

No-one else had seemed willing to intervene, and finally he had snapped, grabbing the towel off the ring-leader and flicking it back at him, until it was he who was cowering on the floor, wailing.

He had walked away in disgust – at the bullies, at the other boys who had stood by and done nothing, and at himself for losing his temper.

Now he was wishing he could go back in time and confront Kat's bullies. It made his heart crease to see her so hurt - his bold, brave Kat.

She was still crying, but more quietly now, tears tracing rivulets down her pale cheeks. At last even those subsided, but she seemed exhausted by the whole traumatic episode. Manoeuvring carefully, he laid her back on the bed.

"You rest here for a while," he murmured. "I have to go and say goodbye to Fedor."

She nodded dumbly, laying her head on the pillow. As he watched, her breathing gradually settled into a deep, even rhythm – she had fallen asleep.

He was reluctant to leave her, but he had to go and see his guests disembark. He glanced back as he opened door. It was the first time he had left a woman asleep on his bed with all her clothes on.

Life was full of surprises.

## CHAPTER NINE

KAT struggled back to wakefulness, not sure why there was a swathe of teal-blue silk beneath her cheek. Her eyes felt full of sand, her throat raw. And she was on a very large bed, in a very large room – not in her narrow bunk down in the cramped crew quarters...

"Ah – you're awake." She twisted sharply at the sound of Javier's voice, sitting up so fast she felt dizzy. "Feeling better?"

"I... um..." Memory had flooded back like a splash of cold water, and she felt her cheeks flame a hot red. "I'm sorry, I..."

He laughed softly, shaking his head. "There's nothing for you to be sorry about. I'm afraid Stasia behaved appallingly. But the family have left now. They went ashore twenty minutes ago. I didn't think you'd be bothered about saying goodbye."

"Oh..."

"I thought you might be hungry. I've arranged for our dinner to be sent up here." That intriguing mouth quirked into a slightly crooked smile. "I thought you may prefer to eat here than down in the crew mess."

Kat hesitated. It was a choice between the devil and the deep blue sea. The crew would be curious – she really wasn't sure that she was ready to face their questions, however friendly.

But staying here with Javier – that was a risk. "I... need the bathroom," she temporised. "I need to wash my face."

The glint of amusement in his dark eyes confirmed that he knew that what she needed was an escape. "I think you know where it is."

She tumbled off the bed, careful not to get too close to him, and darted quickly through the dressing room to that luxurious bathroom she had glimpsed before.

At the sight of the shower she closed her eyes briefly – just the memory of Javier standing in there, naked and wet, brought a hot blush back to her cheeks.

Casting a critical glance at her own reflection in the large mirror above the marble vanity unit, she pulled a face. She looked a mess. Most of her hair had escaped from its knot, falling to her shoulders in a wild mass of corkscrew curls. Her eyes and nose were red – sadly, she wasn't one of those women who could weep prettily.

It was probably perfectly safe to stay here with Javier, she surmised wryly – he was certainly not going to be attracted to her in current state!

A splash of cold water went some way towards reducing the redness of her face, and she borrowed a comb to drag through her hair. She tried to put it up again but her hands felt all fingers and thumbs, so she left it loose, doing her best to make it reasonably tidy.

By the time she ventured back out to the stateroom the sun was setting in streaks of magenta and gold, and a soft evening mist was drifting over the surface of the sea.

Javier was out on the private fore-deck, where a table had been set up beneath the canopy created by the overhang of the main deck above. A row of lights around the edge of the canopy provided a soft glow of illumination, and the deck was protected from the wind by glass panels all round.

The table has been set for two with red napkins and silver cutlery, and glistening wine flutes. As she stepped through the door, a glorious spicy aroma filled her nostrils – spare ribs cooked in Chef's own pepper sauce. She hadn't thought she was hungry, but her appetite was instantly piqued.

Javier was opening a bottle of wine. He glanced up as she slid the door shut behind her. "Hi." He held up the bottle. "Wine?"

"Thank you."

"Sit down," he invited cordially, drawing out a chair for her.

She took the proffered seat a little apprehensively. But his behaviour was impeccably polite – perhaps he was just being kind, to make up for the way Stasia had treated her? Perhaps.

He poured a sparkling froth of wine into her glass, and she picked it up, watching the fine bubbles rising through the pale liquid. "Champagne?" she asked, a little surprised.

"No – it's a Pinot Blanc from the Napa valley. One of the few American wines my father will tolerate." That intriguing mouth quirked into a smile of dry humour. "Which says a great deal for it."

She tried a sip. It was delicious – a delicate, creamy taste, just slightly sweet, with a hint of... strawberries? "Mmm – that's really nice," she approved warmly.

"I'm glad you like it." His smile, and his generally friendly demeanour, seemed quite genuine, and she found herself beginning to relax a little.

A service trolley had been brought up from the galley; the ribs were on a hot-plate, and there was a dish of finely-sliced vegetables and one of croquette potatoes. Javier put some ribs on a plate for her, and passed her the vegetable server.

"Thank you," she murmured – after having served at table for the past few weeks it was quite a novelty to be waited on.

The ribs were as delicious as the aroma had promised – sizzled to a golden brown, the meat so tender that it almost fell off the bone. For a while that was sufficient excuse to eat in silence, but Kat knew she would have to talk to him sooner or later.

The problem was, she couldn't remember how much she had revealed earlier - she didn't want to answer any more questions about her past, in case it triggered a link in his mind with Amy. So far – thank goodness – he seemed quite unaware.

Which perhaps indicated how little attention he had really paid to anything the young girl had said.

A blue velvet dusk was falling as the sun sank below the distant hills to the west. They were leaving the coast of Greece behind, and heading out to the open sea again. "Where are we going?" she asked.

"Back to Antibes. That's the island of Idhra we're just passing. We should be in Antibes by Friday morning."

She nodded, taking another sip of her wine, and sat back in her seat. "I feel like I'm in one of those glamorous adverts, she remarked on a lilt of humour. "*Were you truly wafted here from Paradise?*"

He laughed, catching the allusion. "*These aren't just any spare ribs...*"

"*I don't believe in dicing with danger...*" Ouch – that was a rather sharp reminder that that was exactly what she was doing right now.

One dark eyebrow quirked in amusement. "You don't call bungee jumping dicing with danger?"

"How did you know about that?" she demanded, her eyes wide with surprise.

He smiled disarmingly. "Bob did a little digging."

She focussed on her plate to avoid his eyes. "Bungee jumping isn't dangerous if you know what you're doing."

"I know – I've tried it. White water rafting can be more risky, though."

"Again, not all that dangerous," she insisted. "You need to know the river well - keep hold of your paddle and stay in the boat."

"An excellent metaphor for life!"

She found herself laughing with him. *Careful*, she reminded herself quickly. Don't start thinking you could like him. But nevertheless she felt able to let herself relax a little more - whatever Bob had investigated, he didn't seem to have uncovered the connection with Amy.

"Where are you heading after Antibes?" she asked.

He was sipping his own wine. "I have some business in Nice, then I might drive along the coast to Monte Carlo to have a look in on the preparations for the grand prix. Are you interested in motor racing?"

"I don't know. It looks exciting, but it is a bit noisy."

He laughed. "Well, yes, it is. And it's not much fun if you don't like the smell of high octane fuel and brake dust."

"I prefer the smell of the open sea."

He acknowledge the point with a smile. "I tend to agree."

Kat leaned back in her chair and drew in a long, deep breath, letting the cool, fresh, clean scent of the sea fill her lungs. It smelled of... space, and freedom, and endless possibilities.

It must be wonderful to own a yacht, like Javier, and be able to skim forever across the endless, unbound ocean. No wonder he spent as much time aboard as he could – she would do the same.

"More ribs?"

"Mmm – yes please."

They finished the ribs, then moved the plates from the table to the lower shelf of the service trolley, and took the desert - a delicious tiramisu-flavoured ice-cream, another of chef's specialities.

They had slipped into an easy flow of conversation, rambling over a dozen subjects – music, films, comedians. They found they had similar tastes, tended to laugh at the same things. Kat was struggling to remember the reasons why she should be on her guard. She liked him – she liked him far too much.

They sat sipping their wine, watching as the night sky darkened and the stars came out. They had been out of sight of land for a while, but now there a few lights along the horizon to starboard, and she sensed that they were altering course. Soon they would be leaving Greece behind and heading back across the Mediterranean, back to Antibes.

And then...?

There could never be anything between her and Javier. Letting herself dream that there could be was a very sure way of getting her heart broken.

She had no idea of the time, but guessed that it was almost midnight. But though she knew that she should leave, the temptation to linger was more than she could resist.

Three days. Three days sailing to Antibes. And then...

"You're looking very pensive," he remarked softly.

"I... I was just thinking... It's getting late. I ought to be going."

"You don't have to."

Her breath hitched in her throat. His dark eyes held a question – she knew the answer should be no, but the hunger inside her was stronger than caution, stronger than guilt.

As he came round the table towards her she felt as if she was caught in a spell. The rational part of her mind was clanging with alarm bells - this was wrong, wrong, wrong. But she didn't want to be right. The wicked voice of temptation was whispering inside her head; *Only three days. Why not?*

He took her hand, raising it to his lips and placing a feather-light kiss on the racing pulse inside her wrist. His voice was a husky promise. "Stay here. Stay the night."

Just the way he was looking at her was melting her inside. Those eyes... so dark... dark as sin... He was still holding her hand – she knew she could escape if she wanted to. But she didn't want to.

"You're beautiful," he murmured. "I don't think you know how beautiful you are."

She laughed a little unsteadily. "I think you must have had too much wine."

He shook his head. "Not at all. Your skin is like cream silk, you have the grace of a dancer. And your hair – it's just glorious. The colour of vine-leaves in autumn." He ran his fingers into it, drawing it all to the back of her head, so that she was held prisoner, gazing up into the drowning pools of his eyes.

It would be so good to believe he meant it... *Stop thinking... Just enjoy the moment...* The temptation was aching inside her. And after all, they would be back in Antibes in a couple of days...

Some reckless spirit had caught hold of her. She may be about to make the biggest mistake of her life, but she didn't care. And as his mouth came down on hers, the last traces of her resistance seemed to evaporate. She had no defences left.

All her senses were focused on this moment – with every breath, the subtle musky scent of his skin was intoxicating her, silencing the whispering voice of sanity. His lips were warm and firm, coaxing hers apart; his hot tongue slipped inside, swirling over all the sensitive membranes, seeking all the deep secret corners within.

He was luring her into a magical world of desire, his kiss tender and enticing. With no conscious thought she had lifted her arms to wrap them around his neck, curving her supple body against his, conveying a message he would not mistake.

His marauding hand had slipped beneath her T-shirt, stroking up over her smooth skin, finding the warm, round swell of her breasts. A soft moan escaped her throat as his thumb brushed over the taut, tender nub of her nipple, stirring some ancient instinct, as old as Eve, urging her to surrender.

"Will you stay?" he whispered, huskily soft against her ear.

She closed her eyes, knowing there was only one answer. "Yes..."

With one easy movement he scooped her up in his arms and carried her inside, carried her to the bed.

She stretched like a cat on the silken coverlet. His weight came down beside her, and he drew her close against him again, his mouth closing over hers in a deep, sensuous kiss.

And she could only surrender, everything feminine inside her responding to his urgent male demand.

His tongue was swirling deep into her mouth, exploring all the most secret, sensitive places. His hand stroked down her spine and over the smooth swell of her backside, drawing her closer, making her devastatingly aware of the hard tension of his male arousal.

A small whimper of protest broke from her throat as his lips finally left hers, but it was only to dust scalding kisses over her trembling eyelids and her delicate temple, where a racing pulse beat beneath her skin. Her breathing was ragged, her blood racing in her veins as if she had a fever.

With a subtle movement he eased his fingers beneath her work T-shirt, and a small sigh escaped her throat as she felt his fingers brush against the underside of her breast. The pad of his thumb was teasing at the tender bud of her nipple, stirring a shimmering response inside her.

He grunted his approval as she tugged the T-shirt off impatiently over her head. Damn cheap and sensible cotton underwear, she reflected fleetingly – why couldn't she be wearing something lacy and seductive?

Not that he seemed to notice. With a deftness she didn't care to dwell on, he unhooked her bra with one hand and tossed it aside.

"Did I mention that you have all the essential curves, in exactly the right proportions?" he growled thickly, his hot gaze lingering over the ripe swell of her naked breasts, creamy pale against the slightly richer cream where the sun had kissed her.

She gurgled with laughter. "They're not very big."

"Who needs big?" he argued. "These fit very nicely." He demonstrated by encompassing the whole swell of her breast in one hand, moulding it with his long, strong fingers. "You see?"

She felt the sensitive peak tauten, crushing itself into his palm.

His mouth claimed hers again, drugging her senses. She closed her eyes, letting her hands slide into his hair as their tongues swirled together. She was lost in a kiss that seemed to last a million years - if this was crazy, she no longer wanted to be sane.

This was the only reality, this warm cocoon of pure sensation – his hot mouth on hers, his moist, sinuous tongue invading every deep corner, the feel of satin beneath her, and the warm glow of the light beside the bed bathing them both in gold.

She felt her blood heat to fever pitch as his kisses trailed down the long curve of her throat to find the sensitive spot in the hollow of her shoulder – hot, open-mouthed kisses against her smooth skin, scorching a path over the aching curve of her breasts as she gasped in pleasure, writhing beneath his touch.

The pink buds of her nipples were taut with anticipation as he circled tantalisingly closer, until at last his mouth closed over one exquisitely sensitised peak, grazing it lightly with his hard white teeth, lapping and swirling over it with his hot, moist tongue, suckling it with a deep, sweet rhythm that sizzled along her nerve fibres to pierce her brain.

When he drew back she almost sobbed in frustration, but it was only to unbutton his shirt. She watched from beneath her lashes as he shrugged it aside. She had seen his body before, of course. But the sheer male beauty of that sun-bronzed, hard-muscled torso still took her breath away.

His hand dropped to the waistband of his dark grey cotton chinos, unfastening the button and... phew... sliding down the zip. She sucked in a desperate gasp of air, closing her eyes but then opening them again – she didn't want to miss this.

He was wearing navy blue silk jersey jockey shorts, clinging against his narrow hips and...

She had forgotten to breathe again...

He moved back to the bed, kneeling across her thighs, trapping her half-naked beneath him. His eyes were lit with a hot flame of desire, scorching her creamy skin as he surveyed the territory laid out for his appreciation. She lifted her arms back above her head, wriggling in eager invitation.

"If you keep doing that," he growled darkly, "you're likely to find things move a great deal too quickly."

She laughed, emboldened by the adrenalin racing through her bloodstream. "Maybe I like the sound of that."

"Minx." He hooked his fingertip into the waistband of her shorts. "Maybe you should take these off?" he suggested.

Her heart thudded – she should have known he would call her on that one. But some wicked demon inside her prompted her to respond with a provocative smile, and her hand went to the button at the side of her waistband.

Unfortunately her clumsy fingers rather undermined her attempt to appear cool, as if making love with a gorgeous hunk of male was no big deal for her.

Actually it was her first time – well, her first time with a gorgeous hunk, anyway. One nice-but-dull-almost-fiancé and one persistent-for-a-whole-month-then-vanished-into-the-mist-after-two-weeks didn't really add up to much in the way of experience.

But every girl deserved a treat – and a bruised heart and a guilty conscience were a small price to pay.

"Let me," he offered, his velvet voice straight out of her steamiest fantasy.

He dealt with the impediment in seconds, then he was drawing the shorts down slowly over her slim hips, inch by inch, that beguiling smile teasing her with unspoken promises.

He hooked her knickers as he went, and she lifted her hips to let them pass as he stripped them from her, whipping them down to her ankles and tossing them aside, leaving her naked on the bed.

"I'm not sure if I mentioned this before," he remarked as if making polite conversation, "but your legs were the first thing I noticed about you. They are the most fabulous pair of legs I've ever seen. They start down here..." He picked up one foot, and placed a kiss just below her ankle. "And go all the way up..." He was tracing a hot path of kisses up her calf, past her knee. "To here..." He continued working his way up the inner side of her thigh. "To here..."

Her breath caught in her throat as he reached very top.

"And by the way, I'm so glad you don't go the full Brazilian," he added as he teased his fingers through the crown of russet curls that concealed her most secret places. "I like a little... decoration."

She gurgled with laughter, but then uttered a small gasp as she felt the heat of his breath against her most sensitive hidden membranes. His tongue lapped in, finding the tiny seed-pearl nestled within the folds of crimson velvet, the focus of all her nerve-fibres. Her response ignited, her spine curling as an exquisite sting of pleasure rippled through her.

She was being swept away in a warm tide of sensuality that was melting her bones to honey. A languid sigh purred from her lips as he moved to lie above her, the powerful muscles in his shoulders bunched as he held his weight from crushing her.

For one endless moment the universe seemed to stand still.

"Please..." she whispered, her thighs parting invitingly to surrender her feminine core to the hard thrust of his possession.

She opened her eyes to gaze up at him as they moved to the sensual rhythm he dictated – slowly at first, and then quickening as some elemental force seemed to take control of them both, driving them relentlessly, fast and wild, like tongues of flame dancing together, hotter than the heart of the sun.

She felt as if she was soaring, upward and upward to dizzying heights, the tension coiling inside her, her breathing ragged as her heartbeat raced out of control.

And then a last wild tremor ripped through her, and the cry she heard was her own as she tipped over the edge, tumbling and tumbling, to fall at last into his arms on the wide bed.

♥ ♥ ♥

Kat sat up in bed, resting her chin on her knees. The warm ache in her body was a reminder of the last three incredible nights and two days with Javier. She had never felt so sensuous and feminine – and she had never known that she could respond like that.

And there was no longer any denying it – she had fallen in love with him.

Well, she had done some pretty crazy things in her life, she mused wryly, but this time she had jumped without a safety net!

And then there was Amy... No, she couldn't let herself think about Amy. She was going to hate herself soon enough, but for now it could wait.

They were due to dock at Antibes around lunchtime. Javier had already gone ahead, flying to Nice in his helicopter for a business meeting. He had kissed her goodbye with a flattering show of reluctance, promising to be back later in the afternoon to take her to dinner ashore.

With a deep, sensuous sigh she threw herself back against the pillows again. The subtle musky scent of Javier's skin still lingered there, so that if she closed her eyes she could still see him, still feel the caress of his skilful hands on her naked body, still feel his hot kisses on her tender lips, her breasts, deep between her thighs...

A rap on the door drew her sharply back from the dream. Who on earth...? Reaching for Javier's dark blue silk dressing-gown she quickly shrugged herself into it and tied the belt, and padded over to the door.

It was Gill, with the breakfast trolley.

"Oh... Hi." Kat felt herself blushing a deep pink. She hadn't seen Gill, or any of the crew, since she had come into Javier's suite. Every time any of them had come – to bring their meals, or to clean – she had made sure she was out on the fore-deck, or sometimes in the bathroom.

"Hi." Gill apparently felt as awkward as she did. "I... um... Shall I bring this in?"

"Oh... yes of course." Kat stood back, holding the door open. "Thank you."

Gill wheeled it across the threshold. "Do you want it out on the deck?" she asked.

"No... Um... just leave it there," Kat responded. "Thank you." The trolley was neatly laid for breakfast, as it had been each day, with warm croissants, a dish of butter curls, and a small pot of jam, as well as a pot of coffee.

And lying beside them, her passport. She picked it up quickly. "Where did you get this?"

Gill looked a little surprised at her question. "It was with the others," she explained. "When we're coming in to port, the Captain always radioes ahead with all our details to speed things up when we dock."

"Oh..." Kat nodded slowly. Her passport...

The memory of her own thoughts seemed to echo in her brain: *This couldn't go on - she had to get off the boat, as soon as possible. If only she could find a way to get her passport back...*

Yes – she had to get off the boat, before Javier came back. No more excuses. She had had her fun, now it was time to pay the piper.

"Gill, I need to leave as soon as we dock. Can you help me?"

"Of course." Her friend's eyes were warm with sympathy, and impulsively she gave her a hug. "Oh girl, I warned you."

"I know." Kat hugged her back. "And you were right. That's why I have to leave - I'm not going to wait for him to dump me. But I really need my back-pack."

"Is it a pink one? I know where it is – it's in Javier's office. Do you want me to get it for you?"

"Could you? I don't want you to get into trouble for going in there."

"I'm supposed to go in there," Gill asserted, laughing. "Who do you think does the dusting and cleans the windows? I'll bring it down in a bit – you have your breakfast."

Gill was as good as her word. Kat had just finished her breakfast when there was another tap on the door.

"Here you are. We dock in two hours. Some of us are going ashore for lunch," she added. "Want to come with us?"

"I'll come ashore with you, but not for lunch." Kat smiled regretfully – she was going to miss the new friends she had made. "I need to get to the airport and see how quickly I can get on a flight."

"Right. See you in a bit, then."

Kat swung the pack-pack onto the bed, and unzipped it. It was a relief to have it back – her own clothes, her own toothbrush. Her wallet was there, with a fold of Euro notes and her credit cards, tucked into a side pocket along with her cell-phone – though as she had expected, the battery was flat. Even the pink T-shirt and denim shorts she had worn to hitch along from Barcelona, crammed onto the top.

She had a quick shower, trying not to think of the various uses that facility had been put to over the past few days. Then she dressed in jeans and another T-shirt - they were a little creased from spending a couple of weeks rolled up in the back-pack, but that didn't matter.

Should she leave a note for Javier? But what could she say? Was he even entitled to an explanation? He had enjoyed a couple of days – and nights – of no-strings-attached fun. Which he apparently made a habit of. All she was doing was ending it before he did.

But she did have time to take advantage of being alone in his suite to search properly for Amy's cell-phone. Now, with plenty of light to see by and no need to rush, she could do it systematically.

There were few place where it could be in the lounging or bedroom areas, and she quickly eliminated those. Then she tackled the dressing-room. But though she furkled through every cupboard and drawer, it wasn't there.

Standing in the middle of the room, she drew in a long, deep breath, considering her other options.

The aim of trying to prove that he had had an affair with Amy – beyond those few selfies, which his expensive lawyers could easily brush aside – was to get a court order for a DNA test. So… If she could find something that would have his DNA on it, something that was incontrovertibly his…

Not a piece of clothing – that was all freshly laundered. Ironically, mostly by her! And he didn't wear much in the way of jewellery – just a small signet ring which he never took off. Cufflinks, tie-pins…

And watches. He had several, all beautiful – and all undoubtedly very expensive.

It was risky. First, she wasn't even sure if it would be legally admissible to use evidence taken without consent. And of course, as soon as he realised what she'd done he would likely sic the police onto her.

But with luck, he might not notice for a few days. And as soon as the sample was taken, she would send it back to him.

On balance, it was worth it.

## CHAPTER TEN

"HERE you are, Miss."

Kat opened her eyes as the taxi turned into a leafy avenue. Home. It had been a long and tiring journey. She had hitch-hiked from Antibes to Turin, afraid that Javier would follow her if she went to Nice.

Then she had had a very long wait to get a seat on a plane – it was the week of the Turin Motor Show, and all the flights were fully booked. She had slept in a corner at the airport so as not to miss the chance of a stand-by.

She fumbled in her purse for some cash to pay the driver, then grabbed her rucksack and tumbled out onto the pavement. It had been expensive to get a taxi from Gatwick, but it had been worth it – she had been much too tired to take the train.

She was a little startled to see a smart red sports car parked on the drive. She let herself in, dumped her rucksack in the hall and crossed to the kitchen. Suddenly there was the sound of racing footsteps, and Amy erupted into the room and flung her arms around her neck.

"Kat…!"

"Amy!" She returned the hug. "I'm so sorry I've been away so long without getting in touch. I couldn't ring you…"

"Never mind, never mind," Amy interrupted, fairly bouncing with excitement. "You're back now – and just in time to be my bridesmaid!"

Kat blinked at her in shock. "Your… what?"

"My bridesmaid. I'm getting married next Saturday." She laughed merrily. "Oh, you look like I could knock you down with a feather! But it's true. Jay came back. It was all a silly misunderstanding – well, not a misunderstanding exactly, but he realised he wanted to be with me, and the baby. He told his mother, and she's accepted it. His family are all coming over next Wednesday, to be at the wedding. Oh, I'm so happy."

She flung her arms wide, spinning around the room. "Now you're home everything is just perfect."

A young man had appeared, hovering in the doorway. Tall, athletic build, dark curly hair... a younger version of Javier. Before Kat could question her own sanity, Amy had run over to hug him. "Jay, look who's home! I told you she'd get here. Kat, this is Jay."

Kat stared at him. "You're... Javier de Almanzor?"

That smile – so familiar. "Of course!"

"And in two week's time I will be Mrs.Almanzor. Senora Almanzor. Senora Javier Ronaldo Miguel de Almanzor."

"Oh." Kat sat down heavily on one of the stools at the breakfast bar. Fortunately the love birds were too wrapped up in each other to notice her reaction.

"What did your cousin say?" Amy asked Jay. "Will he be your best man?"

"Yes. I thought at first he would say no." He frowned slightly – another all too familiar expression. "He sounded a little odd."

"Oh, it's the long distance call. And if he's on his boat he might not get a very good signal."

Jay laughed, squeezing her shoulders. "*Querida*, Javier's yacht has all the very latest state-of-the-art equipment. He could probably pick up a signal from the moon."

"Your cousin is called Javier too?" Kat enquired weakly.

"Oh yes. It is a traditional name in our family. We are both named for my grandfather and great-grandfather. We have several other cousins too who share it – we are a very large family. But Javier is my favourite cousin."

"They're all coming over for the wedding," Amy put in. "Well, not *all* of them, not all the aunts and uncles and cousins. But his mum and dad, and all his sisters, and some of the others who can make it at such short notice. Then we're all going back to Spain for big church blessing, and everyone will come to that. He lives near Barcelona. Oh, we have to choose a bridesmaid's dress for you. Let's go shopping tomorrow."

"Fine."

Another footstep heralded the arrival of her mother. "Ah – I thought I heard your voice." More hugs, then her mother stepped back and surveyed her with a critical eye. "Are you OK?" she demanded with that dangerously acute maternal perception. "You're looking a bit peaky."

Kat shook her head, forcing a smile. "I'm just hungry. I haven't eaten anything since some plastic chicken on the plane."

Her mother laughed. "I'll fix you something now. What would you like? I could do you some macaroni cheese?"

"That's fine. Thank you." Kat just sat there, her mind numb. What had she done?

♥ ♥ ♥

With the good fortune which nearly always seemed to smile on Amy, everything had fallen into place. Although it was the height of the wedding season, a last minute cancellation had meant that they had been able to book the perfect venue.

The George Hotel was fabulous, with its wisteria-clad walls and stone terrace overlooking a tranquil lake. That was where the ceremony was to take place, beneath a white wrought-iron pergola.

Amy looked the picture of a radiant bride, with tiny white flowers laced into her gleaming blonde curls, her still-dainty figure set off to perfection by a froth of white lace and a bouquet of creamy white roses in her hand.

"Oh, I'm so excited," Amy breathed, her sapphire blue eyes dancing. "I can't believe this is really happening."

"Nor can I," Kat murmured, glancing towards where the Registrar stood waiting to start the ceremony, the young groom fidgeting and glancing around for his bride, his best man standing like a statue beside him.

Amy slanted her a look of surprised question.

"I mean... it was all..."

Fortunately there was no time for her to dig herself in any deeper. The music had started – Art Garfunkel's silver tones soaring over Troubled Water – and Amy's uncle proffered his arm to lead her down the aisle.

Kat followed.

As they reached the front, and Jay took Amy's hand, Javier turned his head, just once, and looked at her. It was brief, barely a second, but those dark eyes glinted a warning which set her heartbeat racing.

Maybe she should have tried to deal with the issue before. She could have rung him, emailed him – there had been plenty of time. And on Thursday night he had hosted a dinner party here at the hotel, where many of the guests were staying. That would have been the obvious opportunity to speak to him.

But she had chickened out, phoning to claim she was stuck on the motorway, waiting for the rescue service to come out and fix some mysterious fault with her car. In fact she had been hiding in the car park of the local shopping centre.

So she had left it – hoping, maybe, that the presence of all the other guests at the wedding would protect her from the eruption of his anger. Though in her fanciful imagination she had been half expecting him to turn as she had walked down the aisle behind Amy and point at her with an accusing finger: "Thief!"

But all she could do now was stand there in her bridesmaid's dress, like a prisoner in the dock, clutching her nosegay of roses tightly to try to stop her hands from shaking.

How on earth was she going to get through the rest of the day? The wedding breakfast, the speeches, the cutting of the cake. And then... as the chief bridesmaid, she was expected to dance the first dance with the best man.

Javier sipped his champagne, lounging back in his seat. "So, it's done," he murmured in Spanish to his Aunt Mariana, who was seated beside him.

"*Si*. I must admit, I was quite horrified at first. But she seems like a very sweet girl."

"You're not afraid he's got himself caught by a gold digger?"

"Well... At first," she conceded. "But Jay is no fool – I trust his judgement. And they do seem to be very much in love."

"Yes..."

His dark gaze slid along the table. The happy couple were laughing together, caught up in their own sparkling happiness. Next to them, the bride's mother was chatting easily to Jay's father.

Elizabeth Clarke – formerly Elizabeth Tennison. Apparently she had been a shop-girl before she had married Amy's father.

A gold-digger? He had thought so, until he had met her. But even armoured with all his cynical suspicion, he couldn't help liking her. It was easy to see where her daughter had acquired her charm.

Kat.

She was sitting there at the far end of the table, staring straight ahead, a fixed smile curving that wide, so-kissable mouth. But the faint blush of pink in her cheeks told him that she was very aware of his presence.

Those bright copper curls were looped up onto her head with a twist of emerald green ribbon, and her slim shoulders – still a creamy ivory in spite of those long weeks aboard the Serenity – were set off by a dress of emerald green satin wrapped around the slender body he remembered so vividly.

The past couple of weeks had filled with enough confusion to make his head spin. First he had returned to the yacht to find her gone – and no-one would admit to knowing where she was. She had last been seen going ashore for lunch with some of the crew, but she hadn't returned with them.

His instant reaction had been to go after her, but by the time he had found out that she hadn't checked in at either Nice or Cannes airports, pride had got the upper hand. If she wanted to go, then he would damned well let her go.

Then came the first of a series of weird coincidences – a phone call from his young cousin, asking him to be the best man at his wedding.

He had agreed rather absent-mindedly, though after he had ended the call he had registered some concern at the speed of it. But Jay was old enough to know his own mind - though heaven knew how his doting mother would react.

But when Jay had given him the details of the venue, he had been startled to realise that it was in the same town where Kat lived.

And then he had discovered that one of his watches had gone missing. It wasn't one he wore very often – it was a little too opulent for his taste, with his initials picked out in diamonds on the gold face. It had been a gift from a Saudi oil magnate – he had worn it last at the party in Antibes, purely because Abdul would be there, and it was polite to show that a gift was appreciated.

In spite of the distracting events of that evening, he was quite sure that he had replaced the watch in its leather box, in a drawer in his dressing room. But when had gone to select a pair of cufflinks to wear with his dress-shirt for the wedding, he had noticed that some of the things in that drawer were out of place. And the box which should have contained the watch was empty.

He had checked carefully through that drawer and others to make sure it wasn't simply misplaced, but the truth was undeniable. It wasn't there.

So she was just a thief after all. He had cursed himself for being all kinds of a fool.

Although… Why just take the one watch? And one that was so distinctive, that would be very difficult to sell? In that one drawer alone there were several hundred thousands of dollars' worth of jewellery.

And then on Wednesday he had arrived in England, to learn from his young cousin that the deceitful bitch was about to be united with his family through this hasty marriage.

His first instinct had been to warn Jay about the sort of family he was getting involved with. But he had held back. Unlikely as it seemed, it was still possible that he was wrong about Kat – and probably unfair to brand her step-sister with the same brush. He could be wrecking the wedding, and his young cousin's happiness, for nothing.

So now… Apparently it was an English tradition that after the bride and groom had begun the first dance, the best man was expected to lead out the chief bridesmaid.

People were already drifting through into the flower-decked ballroom where a small band were running through their sound-check on a raised dais at one end.

In a few minutes Amy and Jay would take to the floor for their romantic first dance. And then…

Kat was getting desperate. The band had just started to play Amy and Jay's song – Make You Feel My Love – and Jay was coaxing a blushing Amy into his arms. A couple of twirls around the smooth parquet floor, and then…

She looked around quickly for somewhere to hide. Maybe she could escape to the loo…? But as she began to ease her way along the wall towards the side door, she felt a firm grip on her arm.

"Running away? You seem to make a habit of it."

"No… I just… I…" Her heart had leapt into her throat, and she could hardly speak.

"I believe it's expected that we follow the happy couple onto the dance floor," he continued smoothly, drawing her towards that vast empty space beneath the sparkling chandeliers. "Shall we?"

His arm slid around her waist, drawing her close, and she closed her eyes, breathing that familiar musky scent. The music, soft and moody, seemed to wrap around them and she could feel every move of his body as he led her into the dance.

Just as if they were making love...

She had thought that walking away from him had been the hardest thing she had ever done, but this – being with him and knowing that it could only be for this one dance – was even harder.

Her fragile heart, already broken in pieces, was being ground to dust.

She was barely aware that the empty space around them was filling up as more couples took to the floor. She wanted to say something, try to explain, but even if she could have found the words her tongue felt as if it was tied in knots.

It was Javier who finally broke the silence. "I believe you have something of mine?"

"Yes." She lifted her eyes fleetingly, but lowered them again – she couldn't bring herself to meet his granite gaze.

"Do you still have it, or have you sold it?" he challenged. "I hope you got a good price for it – those are real diamonds."

"That's not why I took it," she mumbled against the collar of his jacket.

"Pardon? I can't hear you."

"That's not why I took it," she forced herself to repeat.

"Oh?" The sardonic edge to his voice cut her like a knife. "Would you care to enlighten me?"

She hesitated, struggling to steady her ragged breathing. "It's... complicated."

"We have the whole evening ahead of us," he pointed out dryly.

"I'm not sure where to begin."

"The beginning is often a good place."

Over the past two weeks she had been trying to plan what she would say, but it all sounded so... stupid. And no matter what she said, he wasn't going to believe her. If there had ever been a chance that there could be some kind of future for them, she had blown it – totally and completely.

So she might as well just make some kind of stab at it, even if he laughed in her face – or worse. "What do you know about how Jay and Amy got together?" she asked.

"What's that got to do with it?"

"A lot."

"OK," he conceded. "I know they met in Courchevel. She was working as a chalet host, he was holidaying with a bunch of friends in my Lodge. The season ended, they came back to London together, she found out she was pregnant, they decided to get married."

"You don't know the bit in between?"

"What bit in between?"

"The bit where he turned chicken and ran home to mummy."

It was his turn to hesitate. "No, I didn't know about that," he acknowledged.

"Well, that's what happened. I was in New Zealand at the time – well, you'll know that, you've read my passport. Anyway, Amy rang me. As you can imagine, she was in pieces, so I came straight home."

She risked a glance up at him, to find that he was frowning quizzically. "So what has all that got to do with me?"

"I Googled his name, just to see if I could find out anything about him. And I got you."

"Well, we have the same name," he acknowledged, still puzzled.

"Exactly. If he's even on Google, he'd be on about page five hundred after all the stuff about you. And you have to admit, you do look a lot alike – the only pictures I'd seen of him was a handful of selfies Amy had sent me. Cut the hair, shave off the designer stubble..."

"So you assumed I was your sister's faithless Lothario, and came looking for me?" he surmised accurately. "But why didn't you just say something?"

"Well, so far as I knew, you... I mean Jay, didn't want anything to do with Amy or the baby. He'd just disappeared. And when I met you, you seemed... Well, of course I believed that was what you'd done, and I thought..."

"You thought I was the type to seduce a young girl, and then run away from the consequences?"

"Yes... No... I mean..."

She could feel his chest shaking, and realised that he was laughing. "But why steal my watch?" he asked as she flickered him a look of surprise.

"I wanted to get a DNA test to prove paternity," she explained, not quite sure what he found so funny. "I picked that one because it had your initials on it, so you wouldn't be able to deny it was yours. I was going to send it back."

Now he really was laughing, that rich, velvet sound she had fallen in love with. "That's my Kat." He lifted her off her feet, spinning her around. "Racing off on her wild crusade without thinking twice about it!"

*His* Kat? What was that about? "You believe me?" she questioned uncertainly.

"Of course I believe you. Who could make up such a crazy story as that? I knew the moment I saw you that you were totally unique."

Kat became aware that several heads were turning their way. "Javier, put me down," she hissed. "People are looking at us."

"Who cares?" But he set her back on her feet. It was only a few moments later that she realised he had danced her out onto the terrace.

There were a few people about, but he took her hand in a firm grip and drew down across the wide lawns and through a coppice of trees, until she found herself unexpectedly in the car park.

"Where are you taking me?" she demanded a little breathlessly.

"I'm kidnapping you."

"But... We can't just leave the reception!" she protested. "You're the Best Man, and I'm the Chief Bridesmaid."

"We'll leave them a message," he responded with the bland confidence of one who always did exactly as he pleased. "I thought you might like to have dinner in Paris."

"Paris! But... I don't even have my passport on me!"

"We'll pick it up on the way to the airport."

It was a little after midnight when the helicopter swooped in low over the glittering lights around the harbour at Antibes and landed smoothly on the deck of the Serenity. Javier jumped down before the blades had barely stopped revolving, and lifted Kat down, still in her bridesmaid's dress.

"There. You may regard yourself as well and truly kidnapped!"

She laughed, her head still in a whirl from the events of the past few hours – speeding away from Amy's reception, with just a brief pause at her house to grab her passport, and then flying in Javier's luxuriously comfortable private jet to a small airport just outside of Paris, and dinner in a very exclusive restaurant on the Left Bank, with a view of Notre Dame.

And then waking from a light sleep to glance out of the plane's window, to see ranges of jagged peaks glowing silver-white in the cool moonlight.

"Where are we?" she had demanded, sitting up sharply.

"Flying over the Alps. We should be landing in Cannes in about half-an-hour – the helicopter is waiting for us."

She had turned to stare at him, her mouth open in shock, and he had laughed, taking her chin between his thumb and finger, and leaning over to place a deep, tender kiss on her lips.

She had uttered no protest as he had slipped the zip of her dress and eased the emerald green satin down, leaving her naked apart from a pair of dainty lace briefs.

And then he had drawn her astride his lap, his hot mouth tasting the soft, creamy swell of her breasts, nipping at the tender pink peaks, and had made love to her as the plane purred on quietly through the night.

What could she do? She was his plaything, his mistress, whatever he wanted her to be – and fathoms deep in love with him.

Now, glancing around at the familiar white superstructure of the yacht, she could only smile up at him. "At least you can't claim I'm a stowaway this time!"

"No." He raised her hand to his lips and kissed it. "This time you're home."

*Home?*

But strangely, it felt like home. From below she could hear the sounds of the deckhands making ready to cast off, and walking with Javier down the steps and along the quiet passageways to his suite on the accommodation deck it all felt so… comfortable, so familiar.

Of course it was probably just that the six weeks she had spent here on board had been the longest she had stayed in one place for several years – travelling the world for the tourist company, living out of a back-pack, staying in hostels, constantly on the move. And even when she was at home in Surrey, the house had always felt as if it was really her step-father's, however welcome he had made her.

But she couldn't let herself feel too settled. Who knew how long this might last? A few weeks, a few months…? All she could do was live to the full each day she had – each night. She would have the rest of her life for regrets.

Still holding her hand, Javier drew her out onto the private foredeck to watch as they sailed slowly beneath the flood-lit bastions of Fort Carré and out towards the open sea.

An ice-bucket with a magnum of champagne awaited them, and he deftly uncorked the bottle and spilled the foaming wine into a pair of flute glasses. Handing one to her, he raised his own in a toast.

"To us."

"Yes…" She turned away, not wanting him to see the tears which had sprung to her eyes. Slowly she walked towards the sharp bow, feeling the night wind in her hair. "Look, I…" Something was gripping at her throat, making it difficult to speak. "I just want you to know that… I'm not expecting… I mean, I know it isn't your intention…"

"How do you know what my intention is?" he asked softly, coming up close behind her, his hands on her waist, his breath warm on the nape of her neck.

"I wouldn't want you to think I'm expecting a long-term commitment, or anything like that."

"Are you saying you're just going to have a bit of fun, and then walk away?"

"Yes… I… Not willingly." It was no good – everything inside her was breaking up. "But I…"

"Because you should know that isn't my intention," he murmured. "I want the long-term, the commitment, the wedding ring – the whole damn thing. I love you, Kirsty-Ann Tennison, even if I risk taking my life in my hands every time we have a quarrel. Which I suspect may be quite frequent."

He turned her in his arms.

"So don't even think of walking away from me again. The only way I'd let you do that is if I thought you really wanted to go – but I know you don't." He put up his thumb and gently brushed away the tears that were trembling on her lashes. "I can see it in your eyes, I can taste it in your kisses. This is it - this is us, and always will be."

And when his mouth met hers, she knew it always would be.

# DEAR READER

Hi – I hope you've enjoyed reading about Kat and Javier's voyage of romance. If so, I hope you will enjoy some of my other books – some published by Mills and Boon in the 1980s & 90s, others published more recently direct to you on Amazon.

It's a busy old world out there, and a little froth with a happy ending is a great way to relax and unwind.

**SUMMER SCANDAL** getBook.at/SS-SMC

Annis remembered Theo Lander. When she was sixteen, all the girls in her class used to sigh over him, giggling as they walked home from school past his father's garage, where he worked. Then his father had gone to prison, and Theo had left town.

So what was he doing back here now, nine years later, at her father's funeral?

Theo remembered George Statham's spoiled daughter, with her haughty, high-flown ways. Did she have any idea that her world was about to come crashing down around her? Because Theo had turned the tables on George Statham – and now he owned everything she had thought was hers.

So maybe it would be interesting to stick around after all.

Chasing Stars

# SUMMER SCANDAL

# CHAPTER ONE

"DAMMIT – what the devil's *he* doing here?"

Annis glanced up, startled by Uncle Charles's uncharacteristic outburst. "Who?" she queried, her fine violet-blue eyes scanning over the politely sombre company as they strolled back through the rain towards the line of cars parked on the cemetery's gravel path.

She knew everyone here. None of them were really what you could call friends of her father – a handful of business associates, a few acquaintances from the golf club, here for form's sake as much as anything.

Everyone, except...

"Lander." Uncle Charles muttered the name as if it was a bad taste in his mouth. "I thought we'd seen the last of him nine years ago."

Annis frowned. The name did ring a bell.

"You'll be too young to remember, of course. He used to live around here at one time. Bad family – father went to prison." Uncle Charles had taken her arm, holding his big black umbrella over both of them as he steered her firmly towards the front car. "If you take my advice, my dear, you'll have nothing at all to do with him."

Theo Lander. Yes, she remembered. She remembered very well.

It had been quite a scandal for the respectable little Yorkshire town. But though the name may have slipped back into the mists of half-forgotten memory, the man standing a little apart from the rest of the mourners, apparently reading the cards attached to the impressive display of wreaths, would never fade so obligingly away.

Nine years ago. She had been sixteen, and Theo would have been... oh, somewhere in his early twenties, perhaps. All the girls in her class used to sigh over him, engraving his name in the back of their exercise books, giggling as they walked home from school past his father's garage, where he worked.

In an old T-shirt, stained with oil and stretched taut across his wide shoulders, and a pair of faded jeans which fitted him as if he had been born in them, he was like a magnet for a clutch of silly schoolgirls – all the more of an attraction, perhaps, because he had virtually ignored them.

The other lads who worked in the garage would grin, and try to flirt with them, but they weren't nearly so interesting. It was Theo Lander, leaning over an engine bay or wiping his hands on a piece of old rag, whose notice they had craved and competed over.

And oh, the thrill of those rare occasions when he did spare a fleeting glance in their direction – those dark, dangerous eyes, that blue-black hair curling over the nape of his neck, long enough to be an affront to every anxious parent who had deplored his disruptive effect on their not-so-innocent daughters. Dynamite!

He hadn't changed much, Annis noted, studying him covertly from behind the fine black veil which covered her eyes. His hair was cut rather shorter now, but that had done little to civilise him. Nor had the well-cut black cashmere overcoat he was wearing. Even from this distance she could recognise its quality.

He must have done pretty well for himself since he had left Ridgely, she mused dispassionately, in spite of the scandal which had sent his father to prison. But there was still that intriguing hint of danger about him.

She became aware that he was watching her, and was suddenly glad that she had chosen to wear a hat with a veil, though it had seemed a little over-the-top when she had first tried it on. He was still standing by himself, one hand thrust deep into the pocket of his overcoat, apparently oblivious to the curious stares and covert whispers his presence had aroused.

For one long moment he held her gaze, and she felt an odd little flutter in the pit of her stomach. Dammit, he shouldn't be looking at her like that, as if the slimly-tailored lines of the black silk suit she was wearing revealed rather too much of her slender curves. This was her father's funeral, for goodness' sake!

With an effort of will, she managed to drag her eyes away, but not before she had noted the faintly mocking smile that curved that hard mouth. Yet surely from this distance, and through the shadow of her veil, he couldn't see the betraying hint of colour in her cheeks, nor even know that she was looking in his direction?

But even so, she was conscious that her heart was beating rather too fast. It was ridiculous to let herself react to him like that, she scolded herself impatiently. She was no longer a naïve young schoolgirl, her head stuffed full of romantic nonsense. She was twenty-five years old, and quite accustomed to having men stare at her – and more than capable of dealing with them, too.

Their progress to the car was hampered by people who wanted to shake Annis's hand and say a few conventional words of condolence. "I'm so sorry, my dear. Such a shock for you. But at least it was quick – better than if he had suffered a long illness."

What were you supposed to say under such circumstances? For once she was glad of Uncle Charles's interfering presence as he responded for her, deftly moving each person along after a polite exchange of platitudes. "Thank you. You will come back to the house? Oh, Gerald, a moment, if you have the time – those damned ramblers are demanding we open up that footpath again…"

"Miss Statham?"

She turned sharply. Theo Lander had finished studying the wreaths, and had chosen the exact moment when Uncle Charles was distracted to approach her – not by chance, she was quite sure.

At closer range, she could see the small differences that the years had wrought – a hint of hardness around the mouth which as a teenager she had found so intriguing, matched by a hardness in those dark, level eyes.

That well-cut overcoat, and the expensive patina on his hand-stitched black leather shoes, suggested a discreet aura of wealth – but she didn't think she'd care to speculate on just how that wealth had been acquired.

"Mr.Lander." Somehow she managed to keep her voice cool as she extended a gloved hand in polite greeting.

He accepted her handshake, one dark, level eyebrow arched in question. "You remember me then?"

"Uncle Charles reminded me who you were," she was pleased to be able to retort with some truth, withdrawing her hand from his.

"Ah – of course." That hard mouth curved into a smile of sardonic amusement. "Now I believe I'm supposed to say something about regretting that the occasion of our meeting again should be one of such tragic sorrow."

"I really hope you won't," she retorted sharply.

"Indeed I won't," he conceded. "I know you wouldn't believe any expression of grief on my part. And I can only admire the way you're maintaining your composure. That fetching little veil really doesn't quite conceal the fact that you haven't shed a single tear."

She flashed him an icy glare. It was quite true, of course – her eyes weren't even moist. At her mother's funeral, six years ago, she had cried so much she had thought her heart was being torn out.

But that had been her mother. Now, she would only have cried because it was expected that you should weep at your father's funeral - and she had never been the sort to play those kind of games.

"Lander." Uncle Charles's brusque voice saved her from the necessity of having to think of a response.

"Sir Charles." That cool gaze was transferred, as he held out his hand again. "I'm pleased to meet you. I understand that you're one of the executors of Statham's will?"

"I am." A little to Annis's surprise, the older man refused the proffered hand. "But I fail to see that it's any business of yours."

"Oh, it's very much my business." That smile had an edge of sharpened steel. Theo slipped his hand into the inside pocket of his coat, and drew out a discreetly embossed business card. "You can contact me on any of these numbers. I shall be expecting your call."

And slanting another enigmatic glance at Annis, which flickered down over her slender curves in a way that set her hackles bristling, he turned and strolled casually away towards the line of cars.

"Huh!" Uncle Charles expressed a snort of disgust. "Damned mongrel. Well, he needn't think he can come lording it around here. He may have a bit of money in his pocket now, but he's still nothing more than a second hand car salesman."

**and there's more...**

**CHRISTMAS SECRETS** getBook.at/XS-SMC

Evie was quite sure there must be all sorts of very good reasons why she shouldn't agree to go into a strange house with a man she didn't know. But she had just crashed her car off a mountain road, and it was snowing heavily.

And just at the moment she couldn't think of any alternative which didn't involve freezing to death.

Alessandro Vitucci had been looking forward to a few day's peace and quiet, a chance to get on with a little work while the rest of the world went crazy over the Christmas season. But he had a feeling that his unexpected guest didn't do peace and quiet.


**ROGAN'S GAME** getBook.at/RG-SMC

*Wyoming Terrirtory 1882*
Jake Rogan was a stranger in town – just another gun-toting drifter. But Ella O'Shaughnessy suspected different.

Ella ran the Silver Spur, the town's saloon. And in spite of what the gossips said, she was not – and never would be – Emmett Stroud's mistress.

Emmett owned the Silver Spur. His game was poker – and he played by his own rules.

But what was Rogan's game?

*At 15,000 words, this is either a long short story or a very short novel.*

**and even more…**

These are some of my books which were published by Mills and Boon - these are still available as e-books via my author page on the Mills and Boon website:
**http://www.millsandboon.co.uk/susanne-mccarthy**

Or direct from Amazon:

**SECOND CHANCE FOR LOVE** getBook.at/SCL-SMC
*When handsome country vet Tom Quinn rescued Josey, he had little sympathy for her - wasn't she just another spoiled city-girl like his ex-wife?*

**NO PLACE FOR LOVE** getBook.at/NPL-SMC
*Lacey was **not** having an affair with Sir Clive Fielding. But his arrogant step-son was convinced she was nothing but a gold-digging tramp.*

**FORSAKING ALL OTHERS** getBook.at/FAO-SMC
*It was love at first sight for Maddy when she met Leo Radcliffe – on the night he got engaged to her best friend.*

**BAD INFLUENCE** getBook.at/BI-SMC
*Georgia Geldard was a hard-headed businesswoman with no time for relationships. Least of all with a notorious playboy like Jake Morgan.*

**DANGEROUS ENTANGLEMENT** getBook.at/DE-SMC
*Joanna was a serious Egyptologist. And with mining engineer Alex Marshall ready to start blasting for mineral ores close to her excavation, the last thing she needed was any romantic involvement.*

**PRACTICED DECEIVER** getBook.at/PD-SMC
*The new Lozier Cosmetics contract was a huge opportunity for model Alysha Jones – but it meant working with Ross Elliot. And that would certainly be dicing with danger.*

**GROOM BY ARRANGEMENT** getBook.at/GA-SMC
*Natasha Cole couldn't wait for two years to wrest control of her inheritance from her crooked step-father. But marry Hugh Garratt?*

**SATAN'S CONTRACT**  getBook.at/SC-SMC
*Shaun Morgan had inherited the family fortune. Which left Pippa with few options - people's savings and livelihoods were at stake.*

You can find out more about my books, including those not currently available as ebooks but possibly still in print, from my website: **http://www.susannemccarthy.com**

You will also be able to read some of my short stories (not all of them romances) for free.

I'd really appreciate your feedback and reviews. Come and chat with me on Twitter: **@McCarthySusanne** or visit my Facebook page **on.fb.me/1ygaE4m**

Made in the USA
Charleston, SC
23 July 2015